THE GIRL
WHO DIDN'T
BELIEVE
IN MISTLETOE

THE GIRL
WHO DIDN'T
BELIEVE
IN MISTLETOE

•

MARY LEASK

AVALON BOOKS
THOMAS BOUREGY AND COMPANY, INC.
401 LAFAYETTE STREET
NEW YORK, NEW YORK 10003

PRINTED IN THE UNITED STATES OF AMERICA
ON ACID-FREE PAPER
BY HADDON CRAFTSMEN, SCRANTON, PENNSYLVANIA

This book is dedicated to Bunny, a
valued friend, superb critic and
proofreader, *and* the cats' godmother!

King Street, one of Toronto's oldest, runs parallel to Lake Ontario. It passes through Parkdale, with its older dark-brick houses in the west, and on past the gloomy factories of the garment district. In one glorious block, it blossoms with theaters, a concert hall, and restaurants, then becomes sedate among the elegant glass and granite towers of the business district. For a few blocks near the Farmer's Market, it becomes only slightly fashionable, and then ends in a clutter of old warehouses and factories before disappearing at the Don River. It was along this street that Lucy Allen trudged, hands shoved in her jacket pockets, head down into the cutting east wind, her cloth shopping bag flapping over her arm.

She paused for a moment when she reached the

1

skyscrapers of Bay Street to huddle in the lee of a bank courtyard to get her breath. For the umpteenth time that day, she tried to figure out what she could possibly do to get herself out of the mess she was in. No job, no roof over her head, and worse still, no money. Nothing in her experience had ever prepared her for such an eventuality.

Oh, she had known her temporary teaching job had to end. The principal had warned her the permanent teacher would come back whether she was well enough or not. What Lucy had not counted on was how early the teacher would return to work. Nor had she anticipated her treatment at the hands of her former roommate, Louise.

They never had had anything in common anyway, but sharing the bachelor apartment near the school had allowed Lucy to save money so that she could repay much of her student loan from her days at the university.

Lucy had counted on living with Louise until the end of the school year in June, but when she had arrived home two nights ago, she found her belongings packed up and Louise's new boyfriend firmly established in her place. They had not even offered to help Lucy move her few bags and books. Instead, Louise had waved the rental agreement and said that the fine print allowed her to sublet to anyone she wanted at any time. When Lucy had protested, Louise had blatantly challenged her, demanding whether Lucy would like to be around while she and her boyfriend spent time together. The last straw, however, had been when Louise refused to hand over Lucy's half of the rental deposit, money Lucy had given Louise when they moved in.

For a well-educated girl, I sure was stupid, Lucy thought. *I should have known I needed to sign the rental agreement with Louise, but I let her convince me otherwise. Oh, well, there's no sense wasting energy on that now. I have greater problems.*

Reaching into her jacket pocket, Lucy pulled out some coins; all the money she had in the world, two loonies (dollar coins), a quarter, and a dime. Two dollars and thirty-five cents. Not even enough to pay for a coffee and a Big Mac.

She had started off the day with over two hundred dollars in her jacket pocket, enough, she had thought, to hold her over the few days until she could pick up her check from the Board of Education. But sometime today, someone had managed to slip the folder in which she kept her bills out of her inside jacket pocket. The only place she could think of where this might have occurred was at the coffee shop when she had a muffin and coffee for breakfast. It had been frightfully warm in the building and she had slipped her jacket off her shoulders and onto the back of the chair.

A particularly strong blast of cold air found its way in among the granite pillars, reminding Lucy that she had better walk some more if she was to stay warm. Stepping out into the wind, she wove her way through the busy throng of people going home from work or rushing off to do Christmas shopping, oblivious of the two-storey-high Christmas trees in the bank towers' courtyards and the clusters of decorative lights along the streets.

When she came to Yonge Street, the street that cut Toronto nicely in half by running from Lake Ontario straight north, she eyed the subway longingly. She could hang around in the hallways outside the wickets for a while, but in the end, she still had to make her way east and the sooner she did, the sooner she would be warm. If she could just get over to Sherbourne Street, there was a women's shelter. She was sure there was a McDonald's somewhere in the neighborhood, too, where she could get a hamburger, at least.

Lucy wound her way past a Santa Claus ringing his bell by a plastic bubble in which coins and bills were sitting. *It's a good thing I don't believe in all that Santa mumbo jumbo,* she thought with relief. *At least, Christmas shopping is one thing I don't have to fret about.* Her father had always said, ''Christmas is just an excuse for every businessman in town to get his hands on my money!''

Lucy toiled on, very cold now until she reached the King Edward Hotel. She stopped and looked longingly through the doors at its ornate old lobby and its soft, comfortable chairs. She considered going in and sitting for a while but a look at the patrons caused her to reconsider. She'd look exactly what she was among the smartly suited women and men carrying laptops—unemployed and destitute.

She continued through a small retail section where light spilled out onto the street from colorful boutiques. Lucy tried to distract herself by imagining she was going somewhere exotic in the elegant dresses displayed. Items in a decorating shop caught her eye, and she imagined placing a chair from this window and a curtain from that in her dream apartment.

Then, ahead, Lucy saw the windows of a restaurant she had often admired. She had promised herself that when she had paid off all her loans, she would treat herself to a meal at Chez Paul. She could not resist crossing the street and heading for the window. Just a peek in, she promised herself.

Through the window, Lucy admired the white linen tablecloths and elegant cutlery and china that twinkled in the soft glow of candles. At the back of the room, a glittering Christmas tree stood.

With a sigh, Lucy was about to turn when a wave of dizziness hit. Steadying herself against the windowsill, she took deep breaths. She'd never been dizzy in her life before. Then the desperateness of the situation hit her. She had to eat soon or she was going to be in big trouble. The muffin and coffee had long gone and the cold was using up any spare energy she might muster.

As she pushed herself away, she noticed something on the inside sill of the window. Stepping back, she took another look. A fly, flat on its back with its feet in the air, graced the windowsill of the fashionable Chez Paul.

Lucy took a few more steps along the street and then stopped. The image of a scene in a movie she had once seen came to mind. The heroine had tried to get a free meal by claiming there was a fly in her soup. Could she?

Lucy took a few more steps and her stomach rumbled in protest. Again the wave of dizziness brought her to a halt. She steadied herself against the entrance of the restaurant. Dozens of sayings raced through her mind: *God helps those who help themselves. The Lord will provide.* Nowhere among the sayings did she hear one that said, *No Lucy, this is wrong.*

A particularly cold blast of wind seemed to cut right through her jacket and buffeted her against the entrance. *Even nature is driving me in,* she mused. Shaken by a violent shiver, Lucy made up her mind. She would try. The worst they could do would be to make her do the dishes.

Wood paneling and luscious pots of poinsettias greeted the patron to Chez Paul. Ignoring its grandeur, Lucy crossed the entrance with determination and approached the desk of the maître d'.

It was as if she had donned another persona. Lucy stood proudly, her nose in the air, while the maître d' looked down his at her shabby jeans and running shoes. Staring him in the eye, and in her haughtiest tones, she declared, "A table for one."

With obvious distaste, the maître d' began to lead her to a dark corner, but when she was passing the window, she stopped and in a clear voice stated, "I wish to sit here."

With a racing heart Lucy sat down. She had made it. Nervously, she pulled off her hat and gloves and eased herself out of her jacket. Keeping her head facing straight forward, she swung her eyes to the right to see if the fly was still there. It was, neatly tucked in the corner of the window frame.

The voice of the waiter as he presented her with a large leather menu made her jump. Smiling her thanks, she asked for a glass of water. Immediately, he returned with a cut-glass goblet full of iced water and a basket of warm rolls wrapped in a white linen cloth. *Maybe I should just eat the rolls and drink the water,* she thought. Surely two dollars and thirty-five cents would cover the cost of the rolls.

With trembling hand, she took a roll, lathered it with butter from a small pottery container, and forced herself to nibble politely at it. While she worked her way through the first of the rolls, and there were three still in the basket, she glanced around her. Off in one of the corners was a young couple, obviously in love, exchanging long looks and clicking their wineglasses. Near the entrance, a man dressed in a black leather jacket sat alone. She had the uneasy feeling that he had been watching her. Right before her, but sitting at right angles to her table, were two men.

She found them interesting to study. Certainly watching them was better than wondering if she was going to have enough nerve to order, let alone slip the corpse into the soup.

It was immediately obvious to Lucy that she was looking at a father and son. Both men were extremely tall and long-limbed, and each had the same strong features: firmly drawn jaws, deeply etched smiles under clearly sculpted cheekbones, and heads of hair good enough for any shampoo commercial. Lucy smiled at the thought. These gentlemen, and gentlemen they definitely were, were never going to strut their stuff in a commercial. They were obviously from the upper echelons of Toronto society. Their haircuts alone proclaimed their status. Rich manes of hair, one white and the other golden, were molded to well-shaped heads. She couldn't see their eyes, but she bet they were stunning.

The waiter, a dour young man who spoke with well-articulated tones, returned just as Lucy had been about to slip the other three rolls into her cloth shopping bag. Fearing he might whisk the basket away, she lifted another roll onto her side dish and smiled in what she thought was a thoroughly charming manner. Instead of reacting to her charm, he insisted on reopening the menu and asking if she, Mademoiselle, would like to order. Mademoiselle announced she would need a few more minutes. *I'll call him Fred,* she thought snidely.

As he minced self-importantly away, Lucy realized it was now or never—she would go in a blaze of humiliation before the interested gaze of the blond giant before her, or plunge right into the soup, so to speak.

Glancing at the pair of men, she found the son was still watching her. Hurriedly, she examined the menu. The soup du jour was *champignon.* That sounded good, so when the waiter approached again, she found her decision was made. Mushroom soup it was. However, she refused to be rushed in her next selection, and announced to the waiter that she intended to make an evening of her meal. "After all," she added airily, "what better compliment to the restaurant could *you* think of?"

She thought she caught the son smiling when she made that announcement. She wished he would stop watching her. How was she to set the corpse afloat if there was a witness?

Lucy had just managed to smuggle the two remaining rolls into her bag while father and son were being served their main course when Fred returned with her soup. *Less than two minutes to get it,* she calculated. *They must really want to get rid of me.*

Fred fussed around, making sure she knew which spoon to use by carefully cleaning it on a table napkin. A touch tacky, she thought. Then she heard a gasp. To her horror, he reached around her and removed her corpse. What on earth was she going to do now?

The spoon in her hand suddenly weighed a ton. She was never going to get the nerve to raise a drop of the soup to her mouth. A rumble from her stomach made her reconsider. She had ordered it. She might as well get something in her stomach before she faced the firing squad. She glanced over at the son. He was watching her again, as was the man in the leather jacket. Did she have leaves growing out of her ears, or a nose like Pinocchio for pretending she could afford the place?

This was worse than a gymnastics competition, she thought. At least then she knew basically what she was doing and what the outcome would be. Right now, she was afraid that she would spill the soup, her hand was trembling so much. Straightening her spine, and taking a calming breath, she repeated the mantra she had used in gymnastics. *Focus, think the action through carefully, concentrate.* She dipped the spoon into the creamy mixture and filled it with soup, then carefully brought it to her mouth and emptied its contents. The flavor was definitely worth hanging for, she thought, and was glad she did not live in a century when the penalty for stealing food was just that!

She was about to dip her spoon in again when the sudden grating of a chair on the marble floor of the restaurant made her jump and nearly spill soup all over the tablecloth. Annoyed, she looked to the source of the noise. The golden-haired giant was trying to shove his chair back with his legs while he clutched both his hands to his throat.

Lucy reacted without thought. In a flash she was across to his table. He was still trying to free himself of the chair, still gripping his throat, his face red, the veins in his neck standing out.

Shoving him back into the chair and grabbing his farthest shoulder, Lucy cried, "Turn!" He immediately rotated his back to her. Without hesitation, Lucy slipped her arms under his and wrapped them around his chest. Gripping her hands just beneath his breastbone and pressing her clenched fists into him, she jerked in and up. Nothing happened.

She could feel the stress in the great body. "Please don't pass out," she muttered. "Hold on." Taking a big breath, she concentrated all her energies and yanked her tightly gripped fists inward and up into his diaphragm. She heard the explosive cough she had been praying for, and a missile shot across the room. She felt the expulsion of air as he collapsed against her slight frame. For a moment, he lay there and gasped, then finally straightened up enough to relieve her of his weight and lean against the table.

Crouching by his chair, she loosened his tie and the top buttons on his shirt while he slowly managed to control his frantic gasping.

She glanced over at the father and was frightened to see that he was holding his chest. His color was terrible. Moving quickly to him, she touched his arm. "Easy does it, sir. Your son's all right." Getting up, she soothed him by rubbing his back. "Your son is safe."

She glanced around for assistance. She saw the maître d' rushing from the kitchen and the man in the leather jacket surreptitiously taking something from the floor in his handkerchief and slipping it into his jacket. Fred, instead of being helpful, was fluttering around behind them, saying, "Oh, dear; oh, dear." Turning, she snapped, "Get two glasses of water," and then to the maître d', "The gentleman choked on something he ate. He's all right now."

It was while the maître d' fussed around that Lucy realized that her prayers had been answered. This was just the moment she had been waiting for. If she was quick, she could grab her coat and flee. She knew now that she was not suited for a life of crime. She would rather starve to death.

She started toward her table when a hand gripped her wrist and stopped her mid-stride. Frightened, she turned, expecting that in some way her devious plan had been discovered, only to end up looking into the green, green eyes of the son. Bright color still marred his features and his eyes were rimmed in red, but determination shone out in emerald brilliance at her all the same.

She held her breath, waiting for all to be revealed, for she was sure he must have caught on to her. He rasped, ''Young woman. You just saved my life.'' She nodded dismissively and tried to free herself. ''Please, your name.''

''Lucy,'' and she pleaded with her eyes, *Please, oh please, let me go.*

''Lucy what?''

''Lucy Allen. Please let me go. My soup is getting cold.''

He still held her wrist as if he couldn't let it go. She could tell he needed some kind of release from her. Then, she saw the end of her problems. With a smile that dazzled, she announced, ''If you wish to thank me, you can pay for my supper.'' He nodded and released her arm, and she scurried to her table with relief.

He must have signaled to the maître d', for he followed her to her seat. ''Mademoiselle, I am sure your soup is cold. Shall we begin again? Let me recommend some selections.'' Together, they negotiated a meal the likes of which Lucy had only dreamed. Waiters fussed over her. A new candle was placed on the table. Some flowers appeared. An aperitif was there immediately.

Relaxing for the first time since she had lost her job, Lucy pretended she really was the fine lady she had imagined when she entered the restaurant. Ignoring everyone else in the restaurant, she sipped and tasted, rested and began again, until she finished off with a sinful chocolate concoction named ''Chocolate Profusion'' and several cups of magnificent coffee.

Only once did she return to earth when she became aware of the blond giant coming toward her. Putting down her fork, she cautiously watched him approach. He certainly was a formidable man. There was an arrogance in his carriage that hinted at authority and power. Brushing back his thatch of golden hair—and it truly was golden, Lucy thought irrelevantly, a color most women would kill for—he stopped by her table.

''Forgive me, Ms. Allen, for interrupting your meal. I just want to thank you again for your quick action and for your kindness to my father. He is just recovering from bypass surgery. In fact, this was his first night out. Your soothing manner and reassurance eased his anxiety.'' He paused and watched while she fiddled with her fork. ''You seemed to know what was wrong even before I did.''

Smiling, she explained, "Clutching one's throat and being unable to make a sound are the universal signs of choking."

He nodded. "I realized that you were going to administer the Heimlich maneuver." Smiling, he held out his hand, expecting her to take it. Uneasily, she did, but she found the fair-haired giant unnerving. "Thank you again, Lucy."

He pulled a card from his jacket pocket and presented it to her. Glancing at it, she saw the words *Ross Urquhart, President* and the name of a company famous throughout Canada. "You have only to dial the telephone number on this card and I will be reached at any time, anywhere. My office will be fully alerted that your name will take priority. Please contact me if I can assist you in any way."

With that, he returned to his father, and then left the restaurant. Through the window, she watched them enter a limousine. Glancing around, she noticed that the man in the leather jacket had also departed.

It was ten o'clock when Lucy left Chez Paul's, embarrassed that she had no tip to leave. But the attentions of the staff made it clear that Ross Urquhart had already taken care of this. Standing before the restaurant, the wind cutting through her clothes and pellets of hard sleet beginning to sting her face, Lucy decided to take a streetcar. After all, she still had the two rolls in her bag for breakfast.

Walking briskly to the car stop, she looked back over her shoulder. There was no streetcar in sight. Looking at her watch, she decided she did not have time to wait. With a shiver of apprehension, Lucy began to walk east along the dark and less populated end of King Street.

Ross Urquhart glanced at his watch as he folded his long body into the limousine. Ten-thirty already. What an evening. First, the episode in the restaurant, and then, an unexpected but necessary trip back to his office.

Sighing, he laid back in the soft leather seat and tried to relax. The last thing he had wanted to do was come downtown again after taking his father home, but the security people had felt it was important. A sense of rage and frustration swept over him. Who was doing this to him? He had never felt so helpless.

He yawned and immediately felt the tenderness in his throat. At the memory of the incident, he broke out in a sweat. He'd come so close. Another few seconds and he would have been unconscious. He had already begun to see great dots of light when the young woman had yanked him around and applied the Heimlich.

He could feel her slight, strong arms yet, feel the silk of her hair as it brushed his jaw, and knew the added effort and concentration she had exerted on her second attempt.

Smiling to himself, he remembered that he had watched her enter the restaurant. Quite obviously, the maître d' had wanted to refuse her. His nose had positively curled at her green down jacket, her bright red tam and scarf, faded jeans, and battered runners. But she had stood her ground.

Removing her hat and scarf, she had stood proudly in those long-legged jeans and scruffy running shoes, and said in her haughtiest voice that she wished to dine. When the maître d' had wanted to sit her in a corner, she had firmly insisted on a table by the window.

He had been amused when she had controlled the ordering of her meal and sent the waiter off for water. He was sure he had seen her carefully slipping two or three rolls into her bag.

He had entertained himself with the notion that she might be a bag girl rather than a bag lady, then was ashamed of the idea, for whatever her lot in life, she had sat there proudly, rosy-cheeked from the wind, her cap of hair chestnut-bright in the candlelight.

He had picked up an aura of desperation in her demeanor. He was a good judge of character, quick to size up body language accurately, and he sensed that she was up to something with which she was very uncomfortable. It had crossed his mind that she intended to order a meal she could not pay for.

After the waiter had brought her soup, he had walked around her and removed something from the windowsill. Even in the candlelight, Ross had seen the color drain from her face and her hand tremble as she tried to sip her soup. Smiling wryly to himself, he realized the reason he choked could have been that he had been too busy watching her.

The limo flashed past Chez Paul's and he wondered if Lucy was still there. They proceeded along King Street, past the last of the stores and to a section of dreary warehouses. His businessman's brain wondered if now was the time to invest in some of these properties. It seemed that fashionable Toronto was moving east. The warehouses would make admirable condominiums. He'd have to get in touch with the real estate department tomorrow. As they approached a stoplight, a flurry of motion caught his eye. Three dark figures seemed to be rotating menacingly around someone. As they drove closer, he recognized the red tam. To his horror, he saw a flash of a knife under the streetlight.

He yelled to the driver to stop and yanked open the door as the vehicle screeched to a halt. Springing out, Ross saw Lucy crouched, her arms and fists in a defensive stance, circling, her eyes on the blade of a wicked-looking knife. Even as Ross prepared to spring to her defense, he was startled as

Lucy, in an unexpected explosion of motion, somehow sent the knife flying with her foot and managed to reach the curb, her back to him, her arms braced, daring her attackers to approach again.

Without thinking, Ross caught her around the waist and pulled her into the car. "Drive!" he ordered as she tumbled in on top of him. The car leaped forward while Ross struggled to reach around her and shut the door. Then he steadied her in the corner and regained his seat.

Lucy hadn't a clue what had happened to her. One minute she had been backing toward the road, praying for a miracle. The next moment, she had felt something snake about her body and jerk her backward through the air. She had landed with a thump against a warm body and then felt whatever she was in leap forward. When strong hands straightened her and leaned her against an automobile door, she suddenly realized she was in a limousine.

The voice was familiar. The golden giant! The son! How had *he* gotten into the middle of this terrifying nightmare? A moment ago, she had been eyeing the knife in that very nasty tough's hand and had been quite as afraid as she had ever been in her entire life. And then, she had been flying through the air. Grabbing the armrest of the car, she sat up and tried to figure out just what had happened.

An angry voice barked in her ear. "What on earth

possessed you to walk along the street alone? Are you quite mad?''

If she had been terrified before, she was quite stunned now. It really was Ross Urquhart. How in earth did she end up in Ross Urquhart's car?

Then the memory of the jeers, of the nasty little shoves and the swarming closeness of those creeps, returned. The slicing of that knife, so close it seemed to sear the skin on her arm, echoed in her ear.

Instead of answering the angry voice, Lucy's body reacted to the memories. Her stomach cramped and she felt the rush of bile. *Oh, dear Lord, not here,* she prayed, and grabbed at the door handle with one hand while covering her mouth with the other.

A voice ordered, ''Stop! Unlock the door.'' As the limousine came to a stop, a hand reached out and swung open the door, and Lucy hung out in time to lose every morsel of her heroine's meal: garlic-and-butter escargots, steak Diane, vegetables, and that sinful chocolate dessert.

The final and last humiliation came when the hands of Ross Urquhart held her while she heaved and then hauled her back in and wiped her clammy face with his handkerchief as if it was all in a day's work.

Lying back on the seat, she turned away from him and tried to gather together the shreds of her dignity

although she felt as if it was spewn with her supper
out on the road. But gripping her hands and stiff-
ening her spine could not help the trembling that
overtook her. It took every ounce of will to keep
tears from spilling down her face. Nothing could
keep her teeth from chattering. She muttered without really thinking what she was saying, "I wish I
were dead."

She was shocked to attention when Ross
Urquhart grabbed her arm and turned her toward
him. "No, you don't." And shaking her, he continued, "You were magnificent! You had that bunch
of bullies at your feet."

She stared in amazement at him, then turned
away to hide the sheen of tears that threatened. Ross
watched her in admiration. She certainly had spunk.
For a moment, he was tempted to haul her over and
offer his shoulder for comfort, but he sensed her
dignity had already been diminished too often that
night.

Picking up the car phone, he cued in a number.
When he reached his housekeeper, he issued orders
quietly. "Helen. I need your spare room tonight.
I'm bringing home a young woman who needs your
tender loving care. She has just been attacked by
some ruffians and been sick at her stomach. She is
Lucy Allen, the young woman I told you about. The
one who saved my life."

Glancing at Lucy, he smiled as she attempted to

shrink back into the upholstery. "She probably needs a long, hot bath. She definitely needs some of your chicken soup after the bath. I'll see you in about five minutes."

Lucy was so deep in her misery that she missed the ride through the sedate streets of Rosedale, one of the oldest and most affluent areas of Toronto. She missed the cobbled courtyard of the great stone mansion into which the limousine turned. She was only dimly aware of the strong arm that helped her out of the car or the entrance through the garage into a very large, warm kitchen, obviously from another age but updated with every modern convenience imaginable.

A short, plump, soft-spoken woman named Helen met her at the door and put a kindly arm about her. "Come with me, Lucy. What you need is a nice warm bath, something to eat, and then a good night's sleep."

Bemused, Lucy allowed herself to be led upstairs and into a pleasantly furnished bedroom. She had begun to shiver violently from the cold and her bout of nausea, and stood dumbly while the soft-spoken woman helped her off with her outer clothes.

"Come, child," the woman coaxed, and led her to a bathroom that contained a welcoming Jacuzzi full of steaming water and scented oil. "Leave the rest of your clothes on the stool by the door. I'll pick them up when I have found some nightwear for you. I don't think you should soak too long. I'll call for you.''

In a dream, Lucy finished undressing and eased herself into the water. It felt heavenly. Slowly the aches and pains eased, and she began to drift off to sleep. A knock at the door startled her. The kind woman called as she reached in the door, ''Here is a nightie of mine. It's a trifle short for you but quite warm. I borrowed a housecoat from Mr. Urquhart, Sr. I think you should be able to squeeze your feet into these soft slippers. You step out of the bath now before you fall asleep.''

Lucy quickly soaped herself and shampooed her hair with the wonderful selection of soaps and shampoos provided. Stepping from the bath, she wiped off the moisture with the softest of towels and slipped into the nightgown. Mr. Urquhart, Sr.'s housecoat was of a dull navy-blue silk that, had Lucy known, brought out the color of her eyes. Wrapping another towel around her hair, Lucy returned to the bedroom to find Helen waiting, hair dryer in hand.

''Come and sit down here, Lucy, and I'll dry your hair for you,'' she invited, indicating a stool before the dressing table. Smiling at her in the mirror, she introduced herself. ''I'm Helen Jarvis but everyone calls me Helen, so you must, too. Now, just relax and we'll have your hair dry in a moment.''

Lucy was still too exhausted to exert her

independence. She sat there and let Helen brush her hair under the soothing heat. ''You have wonderful hair, Lucy. The color of polished mahogany. It's so thick and strong and curls around the brush.'' Lucy blushed, for she had little experience of such praise and no experience of such kind treatment.

When her hair was dry, Helen left Lucy to comb it into a style that suited her and went over to the bed to gather up Lucy's clothes. A sudden cry of dismay had Lucy turning toward her. ''My good-ness, would you look at this,'' and Helen held up her jacket, one sleeve out where she could see it. ''Half of the sleeve is sliced through partway up the arm.''

Lucy had survived betrayal when her roommate refused to return her money, hunger and hardship when she had trudged across the city, nerves when she had tried to order her ill-fated meal, and terror when she had met the thugs. But the sight of that damaged sleeve was the last straw. Lucy burst into tears and was gathered into the warm arms of Helen Jarvis. She cried out the events of the day onto Helen's ample bosom while Helen tut-tutted and patted her shaking shoulders until finally her crying ceased. Then Helen got a cloth, gently wiped Lucy's face, talked to her until she was calm, and led her down to the kitchen for some of her famous chicken soup.

As Helen talked to her quietly, a subdued Lucy

sipped her soup at a large pine table. Then Helen brought her over a large mug of warmed milk and returned to her tasks.

Lucy wasn't just sure what it was that made her aware that he was in the room. Some sixth sense and a prickling of sensation at the back of her neck made her turn toward the doorway.

Ross Urquhart was leaning negligently against the door frame, studying her. He had changed into a casual red plaid shirt and blue jeans that snugly fit the longest legs she had ever seen. If Ross was formidable in a business suit, he was lethal in casual dress. In her gymnastic days, Lucy had worked with many young men with gorgeous bodies, but they all faded in comparison to Ross.

His silent scrutiny began to unnerve her. There was something very intent about it, as if she was being weighed for something. Well, he could intimidate someone else, she decided, and stared at him with equal determination.

Ross moved lazily from the door, a smile at the challenge she had sent. She had spirit and he admired that. What he had to decide, however, was whether he had admitted a cuckoo into his nest or a young woman with a perfectly good set of reasons for wandering around in a isolated area of downtown Toronto late at night.

He walked over to the long table and sat himself down at the other end. Deliberately, he brought into sight her cloth shopping bag and placed it on the table. He heard her gasp of indignation as he poured out its contents.

With a long finger, he separated the objects: a comb, a large brown envelope, slightly crumpled, a small plastic bag that appeared to contain some underwear, and a small bag with soap and toothbrush. A small plastic folder contained a driver's license and health card. Finally, there was a zipped bag with a small towel, soap, and a washcloth.

Then he looked at her. For the first time, he was able to really see her eyes, which at this moment glittered angrily. They were unusual eyes, a light, almost blue-gray color with the darkest rim of navy blue around the irises.

She was not so much beautiful as charming. Her face was long, with delicate features, a fine, straight nose, and nicely arched lips. Her crown of shiny hair set off the flush of indignation that he was sure she felt. Good. He wanted her to feel off balance.

Lucy's eyes snapped. "Please, may I have my belongings, Mr. Urquhart."

"Ross," he corrected. "Call me Ross. Surely two people who have saved each other's lives should be on a first-name basis."

"I don't care whether you saved my life or not. It doesn't give you the right to paw through my belongings." He ignored that remark and opened the brown envelope. Carefully he pulled out several copies of her curriculum vitae that she had intended to pass around to local school principals. Now they were all wrinkled.

While she fumed, he carefully read them through. Several times he raised his eyebrows as he read and remarked, "First in your class at York University. Top teaching grades from the Education faculty. A combined degree in Education and Physical Education." He read some more. "A member of the Olympic gymnastic team when you were—" He calculated. "—twelve? Funny, I don't remember your name."

"I was injured just before the games began and the fifth team member had to take my place," she said gruffly.

He looked over at her from those startling green eyes. "Lucy, what was a top student at York, and from the rave references, I gather, a first-rate teacher, doing out on King Street late at night?"

Daring him to comment on her answer, she replied, "I was walking to a women's shelter to stay the night."

He considered her answer, studying her through slightly narrowed eyes. "And what were you doing eating a meal in Chez Paul's with two loonies"—he set down the two dollar coins—"and a quarter and a dime?" He placed them before her. He poked about her belongings with a long finger. "I can see no credit card."

She stared at him defiantly. Wouldn't you just know he would find out how much money she had? Helen must have found the coins when she went to wash her jeans. Finally, she looked down and confessed, ''I intended to put a fly from the windowsill in the soup and demand they give it to me free.''

A look of amused comprehension crossed his face. ''So that's what the waiter removed from the windowsill.''

''No wonder you choked on your food,'' blurted out Lucy. ''Serves you right for not minding your own business.''

He ignored this remark. ''What did you intend to do when your accomplice on the sill disappeared?''

She did not think that was funny. ''Wash dishes.''

Again he gave her one of his green-eyed perusals. She felt like she was being studied by a tiger ready to pounce at the slightest mistake.

''Lucy, why, if you are so gifted as an athlete and a teacher, are you completely broke?'' When she hesitated, he continued, ''There are reasons why I must know. You are going to have to trust me, Lucy.''

She glanced up at the determination and conviction in his face. He had risked his life for her. It stood to reason that she should trust him with her story, although she sensed there was something more to it than she understood.

Pushing her mug away from her, she began to recite the events that led her to her fateful decision to inveigle a meal at Chez Paul's and to risk a late-night walk along King Street.

When she had completed her tale of woe, he stood up. Competently, he packed all her belongings away in her cloth bag, and then, instead of handing it back to her, he tucked it under his arm. "I'll check out your story in the morning and then we'll see where we go from here."

Lucy paled with righteous indignation. She had bared her soul and he didn't believe her. If it was possible for blue-gray eyes to storm, Lucy's stormed at him. "I thought you said I was to trust you. Well, it should work both ways." Standing, she headed toward the door and then realized she was not quite sure where she was going.

A gentle but firm hand took her arm. "Come, I will see you to your room," and he guided her out into the hall and up the stairs toward her bedroom.

Furious, but unable to free herself without a very undignified struggle, Lucy accompanied him. When they reached her door, she turned toward him and sniped, "Be sure to lock the door so I can't walk away with the silver."

Before she could turn back, he completely floored her by reaching up and turning her jaw toward him. "Lucy, Lucy," he scolded lazily. "Relax and have a good night's sleep. Everything will be clear in the morning. I promise you." And then he had the cotton-picking nerve to kiss her. She watched those wicked green eyes glint devilishly as he gave her the sauciest, most teasing kiss in the world, full of impudence and male satisfaction. When he had finished, he opened her door and pushed her inside. As he closed it, he whispered, "Pleasant dreams, Lucy."

Leaving Lucy to fume, Ross made his way jauntily downstairs. The kiss had felt altogether too good, he mused. But it had also made him feel alive for the first time in four years. He prayed that Lucy was real, and that she had no part in the nightmare of events that was haunting him. He prayed, too, that this first thawing of his heart was not just built on wishful thinking.

At the first flush of dawn, Lucy woke in an almost dreamlike state. As she drifted in and out of sleep, she dealt with each of the problems she had to solve. She relived the nasty exchange with Louise and wondered why she had let her get away with keeping her share of the money. Louise taught at the school where Lucy had been working. All Lucy had had to do was threaten to make it known to the principal how unscrupulous Louise was and she was sure she would have paid up. It had been the audacity of Louise's attack that had left Lucy defenseless.

Her mind drifted on to the next problem—employment. Here, Lucy had to admit that she had been avoiding the inevitable. She had known that her supply-teaching job had been running out and refused to do anything about it. She should have been out looking for alternative jobs besides teaching. She could try a gymnastics school, for instance. She would do it first thing in the morning. Having solved those problems, she drifted back into a deep sleep.

Lucy awoke with a start. Very bright light was shining in her eyes. Glancing at her watch, she gasped. Ten-thirty! She never slept in, never. Throwing back the covers, she sprang out of bed only to feel just a little bit muzzy. *Strange,* she thought. *I didn't hit my head last night but I feel a little disoriented.*

She walked over to the window. It overlooked a cobbled courtyard surrounded by a stone wall and griffin-guarded entrance. As she studied the scene, a limousine entered the courtyard. To her amazement, the leather-jacketed diner of the previous night hopped out of the driver's door and walked briskly around toward the passenger side. But before he reached it, Ross Urquhart sprang out. Two other men came out of the garage, and the four of them appeared to hold a conference. As they talked, they seemed to be studying the building, pointing at the roof and areas beyond her range of sight.

Finally, with a glance upward toward her bedroom window, Ross strode toward the house.

Lucy continued to stand at the window, safe from discovery behind the curtains, lost in thought. Last night, she had felt there was something going on. She was even more convinced today. What was the man in the leather jacket doing driving the limousine? Why did she think that a limousine was hardly Ross Urquhart's style? Why did Ross have to check out her credentials? After all, she would have had no way of knowing he would be seeing her curriculum vitae, so it had to have seemed genuine to him. And why did she now begin to have the niggling idea that someone, Helen, for example, had put something in her milk to make her sleep? That notion made her very uneasy. She had been touched by the housekeeper's kindness. To believe her capable of deceit was disillusioning and rather frightening. It meant that there was no one she could trust in the house.

Glancing around, Lucy found her clothes, newly washed and pressed, sitting on a chair. She showered and dressed as quickly as she could, determined to go downstairs and get some answers.

Her plans to quiz Helen were quickly scuttled when she found Ross sitting at the pine table, a cup of coffee in one hand and the newspaper spread before him on the table. At her entrance, he smiled, and stood to pull back a chair for her. "Good morning, Lucy.'' Glancing at his watch, he raised an eyebrow and smiled. ''You must have had a good sleep. It's eleven o'clock.''

Good sleep, my foot, she thought, and sat down in the proffered chair.

Helen called from the kitchen area, ''I'm just making Ross some French toast with maple syrup and crisp bacon. Want some?''

Visions of several days ahead with little or no breakfast forced Lucy to say she did, but her compliance angered her. She really did not want to eat any more of this man's food until she knew what was going on.

She glanced over at him. He was watching her with the satisfied smirk of a cat who had just seen his next meal. What on earth had he to grin at? she wondered, and then she remembered—*the kiss,* something that her subconscious had carefully hidden from her until that very moment.

To Lucy's annoyance, she felt a blush sweep over her. Burying her nose in a glass of orange juice, she gulped it all down, probably almost killing her system with an overdose of sugar, she thought grimly.

She glowered over at her companion, watching him consume enough French toast to feed an entire shelter full of women, and her father's voice went off in her head. *''The rich don't know what life is really like. They're born with silver spoons in their mouths. They don't work. They just sit around and enjoy the fruits of other people's labor.''* She hushed the voice, for as an adult, she knew that her father had had a chip on his shoulder. Probably with good cause. He had been left with an infant girl to raise when her mother died, and had to work long, hard hours to provide for her and her training.

Ross looked up and found her watching him. ''Eat up, Lucy,'' he ordered. ''And then we'll go to my study. I have some things I want to discuss with you.''

In spite of her distrust of him, and even of the kindly housekeeper, a taste of Helen's French toast had her hooked, and she cleaned up a second helping swimming with maple syrup. *After all,* she thought ungraciously, *I might as well enjoy the maple syrup while I can. We regular mortals can't afford the real thing.*

Ross waited patiently for her, and when she had finished, invited her to follow him. Thanking Helen for the magnificent breakfast, she followed him down a corridor in the opposite direction from the night before. They reached a heavy door and Ross reached around her, opened it, and invited her to enter.

Lucy stopped in astonishment. Talk about ''America's Castles.'' This had to be the Canadian equivalent. Before her was a formal entrance to the house that equaled any found in a baronial estate in the old country. A fabulous black-and-white tiled floor, rich, dark-paneled walls, and a great stone staircase climbing one wall and forming a minstrel gallery across the back all faded against the magnificence of an incredible stained-glass wall that faced the entrance doors. The light filtered in through the glass, outlining the shape of the minstrel gallery and casting jewels of rainbow hues across the tiled floor.

Glancing up, she could see the ceiling was arched with the same glowing wood. The only thing that marred its grandeur was a thin, flat pair of metal struts that crisscrossed the expanse. Lucy could not stop the irreverent thought that they would make excellent balance beams on which to practice, as long as one didn't fall off. Their height and the tile floor below almost guaranteed bashing one's brains in.

He caught the tiny smirk when she looked up. "What are you thinking of, Lucy?" And then he amazed her by reading her mind. "Balance beam, perhaps? Not a chance." He surprised her again by turning her toward him and demanding, "Promise me, Lucy, that you will never put a foot, or hand, for that matter, on those struts."

She couldn't see why he was getting into such a snit. It wasn't as if she was going to be there long enough to be tempted. With a shrug, she promised.

He guided her across the entrance hall while explaining that his great-great-grandfather had built the house, and in particular the entrance, to establish in the minds of the Toronto gentry of that period that a man who began with little formal education and no family background could accomplish everything they had and more. Consequently, he explained, everything in the house was just a little larger than life, as she would soon see.

He guided her down another corridor to a room that looked out the back of the house. Again, Lucy had the strange feeling that she had stepped into another time, or a movie set at MGM. This was obviously the library. On three sides, the high-ceilinged room's walls were completely covered with shelves full of books, many leather-bound. There was even a ladder suspended from a runner on top of the cases.

At one end, the wall was filled by a tremendous stone fireplace incongruously updated with glass doors and a gas fire. Over the fireplace hung the picture of a bewhiskered gentleman who could only have been the great-great-grandfather. Near the fireplace, a large desk was obviously in use and on another, a bank of business machines resided.

Before the fireplace sat a pair of comfortable armchairs and a chesterfield. Walking over to them, Ross invited Lucy to sit down and then went over to the desk to pick up a folder.

Lucy watched, trying to forget her curiosity about the house and focus her suspicions. He graced her with another dynamite smile, and sat down opposite her, crossing those long, long legs of his. Today, he was back in a beautifully cut gray business suit. Lucy suspected he had been at work for hours before returning to settle with her.

Ross opened the folder, picked up a set of papers, and handed them to her. Glancing down, she discovered that they were sets of her curriculum vitae, exquisitely printed.

"Lucy." He waited until she looked at him. "I am sorry I found it necessary to check out all the facts. If it had been only my safety to consider, I would have taken your word as truth; however, there are other people involved."

"Safety?" she echoed. "Other people?"

Standing up, he reached across to her and offered her his hand. She seemed to have no choice but to take it. He pulled her to her feet and led her over to beautiful diamond-leaded windows. As she went, she became aware of the sound of children's voices.

Below them on an grassy space with nets set at each end were two children playing hockey. A redheaded boy, about eight, she guessed, and an equally redheaded girl about six, were passing a ball back and forth with hockey sticks. She was amused to note the small child was holding her own with what could only be her brother.

"These are my children, Lucy." He said no more, but stood watching them.

She waited for more information. When finally she could stand the silence no longer, she blurted out, "Where is their mother?" Now why on earth had she asked that? she wondered, and blushed.

"Their mother died four years ago, when Amy was only two. They are the most precious things in the world to me. All these signs of wealth you see around you are nothing, Lucy, without them, and I would trade it all for their safety."

"You keep mentioning safety. Is there a problem?"

"There have been written threats on my life, and two attempts. The first was on the subway. I live so near work that I often walk up to the subway and take it downtown." She could not help raising her eyes at this. "You're surprised, Lucy?"

Embarrassed, she shrugged.

"I like riding the subway. I go to work very early so I miss the crowds. Because of the children, I return home early in the afternoon. I can work from here if necessary. When they have gone to bed, I can return to work. I also have a personal assistant who spends quite a lot of time out here."

He let that sink in and then continued, "I really am a very ordinary person, Lucy. I have the same values as other men. I love my family. I enjoy my work and take it seriously. That's why I find this harassment so frightening. Someone is intent on doing harm to me, and now my children. Neither the police, my security firm, the detective agency I've hired, nor myself can figure out who is doing the threatening.''

"You said that there were two attempts on your life?"

"Yes. As I started to say, the first occurred when someone deliberately tried to push me in front of a subway train. Only the fact that I weigh a lot and was able to resist the force of the push saved me. The man who pushed was up the stairs and out of sight before I could quite grasp what had happened. It was a bold attempt, made on the platform when there was hardly anyone there. No one noticed anything because the train drowned out my shouts.''

Lucy shuddered.

"You might well shudder, Lucy. It scared the wits out of me. Until then, we had been ignoring the threats. People in my position get them all the time.''

He continued, "I started to drive my car to work. A few days later, while I was on the expressway, I put my foot on the brakes to slow down when someone cut in, and they failed. Luckily, no one was hurt, as I was able to whip the car onto the shoulder.

"But yesterday, I got another note, this time warning me that my children had better watch themselves while they walked to school.''

Lucy felt her own stomach turn as she watched

the two below her, struggling over the ball with their sticks.

"Lucy, I want to employ you as their teacher and their guard. I will pay you exactly what you would have earned as a full-time teacher with two years' experience. I will pay all the benefits you would enjoy if you were working for the Toronto Board of Education. Your salary will continue until the danger is over and until you have found a suitable long-term teaching job."

When Lucy looked at him, her mouth literally hanging open with surprise, he continued, "I can't risk letting them go to school, and there are still eight days of classes before the Christmas holidays. I need someone who has sufficient energy to keep up with them. As you can see, they are both competitive to a fault. Such drive needs focusing."

Leading her back to the chairs, he said, "I gather from your training that you are qualified to teach them, so they won't get behind in their lessons, although that is not my main concern. They are at the top of their classes and a few days' absence would not hold them back. What really concerns me is that they will miss all the fun of getting ready for Christmas."

Lucy's heart sank. Even as her wildest hopes seemed to be answered, she realized she had to be honest. She could hear her father's voice. *"Christmas and Santa Claus and all that stuff is for chumps. The only Christmas spirit about is the spirit of greed.''*

Lucy paled but felt she had to say it. ''I have to be honest with you. I don't believe in Santa Claus and mistletoe and all that stuff.''

That was not what he wanted to hear. Already, he had graced Lucy with characteristics that did not include such cynicism. ''Didn't you ever hang up your stocking at Christmastime or buy presents for your family?''

Lucy looked uncomfortable. ''My father did not believe in Santa Claus or giving gifts.''

''And your mother?''

''My mother died when I was an infant. I was raised by my father.''

''And where is he now, Lucy?''

''When I graduated from high school, he got a chance to work in Australia. He had always wanted to travel, to start a new life, he said, so he went to Australia. He doesn't plan to return.''

To say this out loud hurt Lucy as it had hurt her when she realized that Ronald Allen had resented being tied down by her. He had washed his hands of her except for the cost of her tuition fees, sure that she would succeed at university on scholarships and with summer jobs. He'd said he'd prepared her well to face any eventuality. *I wish he could have been around last night,* she thought bitterly.

If Ross was shocked at her revelations, he

covered it well. "I think, Lucy, if you will give me your word of honor that you will treat all the children's Christmas activities as if you did believe in them, then you are still the person I want to trust them with."

Her eyes flew to his. Such trust moved her. In spite of herself, she felt tears gather in her eyes and turned away to watch the children again. No one in her life had ever trusted her with such confidence. "I would do my best," she answered gruffly. "But you may have to help me with Christmas and all that."

He studied her pale profile, surprised at the tears. "There's more, Lucy. I also want you to keep an eye on my father. I want him to feel free to go about but I don't want him to be put at risk. I've explained matters to him after last night."

"Last night?"

"Yes, when I choked on the food."

The light dawned. "That's why your chauffeur grabbed the bit of food and smuggled it away."

"You're observant as well as quick-thinking, Lucy. You're right. It turned out there was a small bone in the food, something Chez Paul's was embarrassed to discover. However, there is no evidence of deliberate tinkering with the meal. It was just a case of carelessness.

"Kevin, the chauffeur," he added, "is the head of a team of men and women who have been hired to try to ensure my safety. I will introduce you to them if you agree to take the job.'' He watched her for a moment as she considered. ''Well, Lucy, what do you think? There may be danger in it for you. Are you willing?''

This time, she held out her hand without worrying about contact with him. He took her hand in his great paw, and she said quietly, ''I will do my best.''

Obviously pleased with her reply, he turned and headed for the door. ''Come on. I'll introduce you to the children. By the way, I've had to explain to them about the threats so they would understand why they couldn't go to school.'' And then, as an afterthought, he asked, ''What was it you did to knock the knife out of that hoodlum's hand last night?''

With a cocky grin, she informed him, ''Tae kwon do. I'm a black belt.''

He surprised her by laughing, putting his arm around her shoulder, and leading her down the hall. ''You're full of surprises, Lucy. I am positive you are just what this household needs.''

By the time they reached the kitchen, the children had completed their hockey game and were sitting around the table having lunch. They had been joined by their grandfather and Helen.

It was evident to Lucy that the children were not used to their father bringing a stranger into the kitchen, because they immediately stopped eating and watched her carefully. Ross's hand on her back guided her forward. "Kids," he announced. "I'd like you to meet Ms. Allen. She has agreed to be your teacher until the new year." That brought exactly no response. Instead, the children still sat, their sandwiches still in their hands, sizing her up, and, Lucy was sure, thinking, *Why on earth do we need a teacher until the new year?*

Indicating his father, Ross said, "Ms. Allen, you remember my father." Lucy smiled shyly at the older gentleman. Gesturing toward his children, he continued, "I'd like you to meet my daughter, Amy, and my son, Robbie."

Both children put down their food, got up, and politely made their way to her, where they offered their hands. *Nicely trained in the formalities,* Lucy thought, and accepted each of their small hands. "It's nice to meet you. I was watching you play hockey. You're very good with the hockey sticks."

"I play hockey with the Rosedale Midgets," Robbie announced proudly.

"Can you play hockey?" asked Amy, her bright blue eyes sparkling with interest.

"I'm afraid I was never lucky enough to have a brother, so there was no one to play hockey with. However, I did take some figure skating lessons."

Ross steered the children back to their seats.

When Robbie settled, he announced, ''Figure skating is for girls.''

Uh-oh, thought Lucy. *I guess that puts me in my place.*

''Are you sure, Robbie?'' asked Ross. ''What about Elvis Stoyko, Todd Eldridge, and Kurt Browning? You enjoyed watching them skate.''

''Yes, but they did boys' skating.''

''Well,'' said Ross, ''I seem to remember both the women and the men doing spins and jumps.''

Very nicely done, thought Lucy. *He's expanding the child's information without putting him down.*

''Would you like to learn to do some figure skating, Robbie?'' asked Ross. ''I understand some hockey players have studied it to give them more flexibility. Maybe Ms. Allen could teach you while she is here.''

But I have no skates, thought Lucy.

Ross continued, ''You might be interested to know that Ms. Allen, who I think we might address as Lucy if she doesn't mind, is also a gymnast. I was wondering if we should get some equipment so that she could teach you the basic skills of gymnastics also. After all, it is nearly Christmas. You don't want to be doing regular schoolwork all the time. What do you think, Lucy?''

I think you like getting your own way, thought Lucy. However, she smiled and said to the children, ''I would be glad to teach you gymnastics. I would also enjoy sharing with you the little I know about figure skating, but only on condition that you teach me how to play hockey.''

Then with a smile, she turned to Ross. ''If the temperature drops, maybe we can flood the grass where the children were playing today.'' As an afterthought, she added, ''Maybe you can play hockey, too.''

She had said that to annoy him, for it had aggravated her that he had set up everything with the children without first asking her advice. Glancing up, she met his very wicked green gaze and knew that he was aware that he had annoyed her, and understood exactly what she was up to.

Giving one of his smug cat smiles, he agreed. ''Sounds like we'll all have to check our skates. I think that you'll both need new ones. Maybe Lucy can take you over to the sports shop to get you fitted tomorrow. Now, you'd better eat up.''

They left the children, Helen, and their grandfather, but not before Ross reminded the children again of the new safety rules they were to follow. He took the opportunity to stress that they were to follow Lucy's instructions at all times when they were with her.

Later that night, Lucy stood, bemused, in the middle of the room that was to be hers. Again, she had the sense of experiencing a time warp, for before her in all its glory was a magnificent mahogany four-poster bed with soft brocade canopy and curtains. Heaped on top of the bed was a duvet cover of finest cotton percale and delicate lace, and piled at the head of the bed was an equally delightful cluster of lace-trimmed pillows.

Walking over to the bed, Lucy sat, closed her eyes, and tried to gather her wits together.

It all had started when Ross had led her back to the library. When he had settled them in the chairs by the fire, he took a notepad from the table in front of them and began to go over a list he had obviously planned some time before.

"Just out of curiosity, Lucy, and before we start discussing your specific duties, can you explain to me how it is that you left the high school you were at last year to teach on the supply list in elementary school this year?"

So he was checking again, she thought. However, she answered equably enough, "I was hired full time to teach physical education at a high school, but with the provincial cutbacks during the year, all the new teachers were let go in June. Since I was qualified to teach both elementary and secondary school . . ." He raised an eyebrow at this. "I had taken extra courses to make sure that I could work at both levels," she explained. "Anyway, a supply-teaching job came up in the elementary panel first and I took it. I quite enjoyed working with the grades four to eight in the gym program.''

Her answer seemed to satisfy him, for he referred back to his list and asked, ''What do you think would be a good organization of the children's time over the next school days?''

She had been thinking of that during the past half hour. ''I have some suggestions. First, I think it would be best to keep the academic work to a minimum. You said they are well ahead of their classmates. I'd like to suggest that aside from regular time to write and read, they spend their time learning something different.''

She watched his rugged features, expecting a frown of disagreement. Instead, she received a smile. ''I agree with you. What things would you suggest?''

''Well, you have already suggested gymnastics and I think that's a good idea. But you would have to get some equipment.''

He nodded in agreement.

''But where would we work?'' she asked.

''How about the entrance hall? There is certainly room for handstands and somersaults, and any other feats of daring you can imagine. Again, I would expect you to use your judgment so that no harm came to the window or the furnishings. And no work on the wall supports,'' he teased.

She chose to ignore this. ''I was half-kidding

when I mentioned flooding the grass to make a rink. Wouldn't it have to snow some and become colder before a rink could be made?''

He flashed her one of his green-eyed smiles. ''The temperature is dropping to well below freezing tonight. It is also expected to snow quite heavily. By tomorrow night at the latest, we should have a foundation on which to flood the rink.''

The thought of skating made Lucy feel uncomfortable. She did not have skates nor the money with which to buy them.

He watched her while she fidgeted. He noticed the flush on her face and the way she looked around as if gathering the courage to say something. ''What's wrong, Lucy? Are you changing your mind?''

Surprised, she shook her head. ''Of course not. It's just that I don't have a pair of skates.''

''That's no problem. When you take the children to get their skates and any new skating clothes they need, you can also select a pair of skates and any other things you require. You'll need ski pants, a skating skirt if you are to keep up with my daughter, and, of course—'' He paused with a smirk. ''—a hockey stick if you intend to beat me. Be sure you get good equipment, Lucy. Choose skates that will last you a good number of years.'' When she started to protest, he waved her silent. ''The skates are necessary equipment and will be purchased from the same budget you use to get all the other sports equipment. I think you should take the children tomorrow. After supper tonight, I will suggest where you should go. Kevin can take the three of you in one of the cars. He'll drive you home when you're finished.''

Ross had continued down his list, efficiently clarifying all of Lucy's duties and responsibilities. They both agreed that she would have little time for herself until the danger was over; however, Lucy was not particularly troubled by this. Watching the children gave her something constructive to do during a season she often found very lonely.

The gentle sound of snow hissing on the windowpanes brought Lucy back to the present. She walked over to one of the two long windows in the high-ceilinged room and watched the scene outside. She found she was overlooking the open area where the children had played hockey. The space was lit up with security lights so that the snow drifted in gentle clouds across the space. It was evident that the property dipped down behind the playground into the ravine. The swirling snow settled on the trees, creating ghostly shapes against the dark night.

The hiss of flakes against the glass made her shiver and she remembered her torn jacket. Ross had insisted that he get her a new one. When she had been stubborn about this, he simply called Helen to tell her to let him know the size of the damaged jacket and then telephoned someone in his office with instructions to go to a well-known sports outfitter, one she would never have dreamed of using, and get her a new jacket. He even insisted that the jacket be a deep green.

Leaving the window, Lucy wandered on around the room and stopped before a beautiful mahogany dressing table and chair. On the table sat an elegant glass tray with a collection of expensive creams and lotions. She had received instructions, when Ross had led her to this bedroom door, that they were for her.

Lucy continued her tour. There was a walk-in closet almost as large as the tiny bedroom she had had in her old apartment. She gasped with astonishment, for not only were her clothes from the commercial locker in which she had stored them in the closet, but also clothes from a trunk she had left with a friend. She shook her head in wonder. She had given the tags for the clothes in the locker to Ross along with a written authorization for her friend to give an employee of Ross's her trunk only that afternoon, and they were already here and stowed away. The new green jacket was also hanging there.

She hurried over to an elegant dresser only to find it full of her things. Poor Helen must have been very busy, she thought.

Lucy completed her tour by examining the en

suite bathroom. Again, she felt a sense of time slipping around her in some unmanageable way. The bathroom was an interesting combination of Victorian and modern design. In fact, Lucy thought humorously, it was a bathroom to die for. There was a glassed-in shower with multiple jets, a very long, elegant ceramic tub raised on brass claws, a madly ornate marble dressing table, and beautiful china fixtures.

Unable to resist the temptation of another soak, Lucy gave herself up to the joy of lolling in fragrantly scented water while her still-tired muscles relaxed after the previous day's harrowing experiences. Settling herself back against the tub, she reviewed the events of the last thirty-six hours. But mostly, she thought of her employer.

Ross Urquhart was truly new to her experience. Here was the kind of man she had read about in the business magazines: successful, powerful, and quite used to getting his own way. She was uncomfortably aware that there was a physical attraction between them, something she did not want. She had promised herself that she would depend on no one again since her father had left her so abruptly. It hurt too much.

Lucy turned on the tub's tap and added some hot water. She found herself thinking of her father. As they had walked back to the study, Ross had remarked that her father must have been a very committed parent if he had taken her to gymnastics classes and then figure skating lessons. It went without saying that he had spent all his money on her lessons. Lucy squirmed at the thought. She had felt so betrayed when her father left that she had not spent a lot of time wondering how her father had made ends meet over the years. Nor had she wondered about his social life.

Her father still wrote her every Christmas but she had refused to answer him. For the first time, her behavior seemed childish and selfish. Trust Ross Urquhart to make her feel guilty.

Then her memory of the events at her bedroom door tonight made her grin. Ross had walked her upstairs in the wing of the house above the library. He had shown her the children's rooms, next door to hers. He had also indicated that his rooms were in the suite at the end of the hall beyond the children's rooms and that his father's suite of rooms was opposite hers.

But his eyes had sparkled devilment the entire time he had explained this. He knew very well she was remembering the saucy kiss he had bestowed the night before. He knew that she was on her guard in case he tried something like that again. Instead, he opened the door for her, remarked that with his father's rooms right across the hall, she would be well chaperoned in this wing, and left, whistling softly to himself.

*   *   *

Lucy found Ross Urquhart's children quite amusing. Robbie was very like his father, she decided. They had no sooner settled in the car than Robbie was going over a list he had made of things he thought they needed at the sports store. In these items were included things for his sister. He had even asked Lucy about the kinds of things she needed.

Amy, on the other hand, was in love with the thought of trying on figure skates, and of course, a skating costume. Amy also stated quite decisively that she wanted all-purpose skates for hockey. When Lucy had looked surprised at this, Robbie had agreed that Amy would need two kinds of skates, all-purpose as well as figure.

Although it was a weekday morning, the store was still quite busy due to a storewide sale of ski equipment. In spite of that they all had fun trying on their skates. A salesman was only too glad to sell them four pairs of skates and help them get the correct hockey sticks and pads.

It was while Amy and she were trying on skating outfits that Lucy suddenly realized that she had lost sight of the little girl. Amy had finished dressing and had left the cubicle with her skating skirt ahead of Lucy. When Lucy had finished dressing and come out, Amy was nowhere to be seen.

Fear squeezed her heart. "Where's your sister?" she demanded of Robbie.

Robbie looked surprised and glanced around. "She was right here a moment ago."

Frantically, Lucy began to search up and down the rows. With each second that passed, she was more sure something had happened to her. Amy was so small that it was impossible to tell if she was on the other side of the rows of sports equipment.

Lucy was just about ready to call the manager when Amy's voice called behind her, "Lucy. Come and see what I've picked out for Grandpa."

Spinning around, she found a gap-toothed Amy, all smiles, holding up a knitted ear-warmer, the kind one pulled on over one's head. Almost trembling with relief, Lucy found it all she could do to curb the urge to shake the child. Taking a slow breath, she knelt before Amy and took her gently by the shoulders. "Amy. You must not leave without telling me where you are going."

Amy opened her mouth to protest but Lucy continued. "Do you remember what your daddy said about staying with me at all times? He meant in the store, too. Do you understand?"

Amy understood all too well that Lucy was upset, and nodded her agreement. Remembering the gift for her grandpa, she shoved it at Lucy. "I bought this for Grandpa. He said if it isn't too cold he would come out and be the umpire when we skate with you and Daddy.''

Lucy let the event pass but when they were back in the car, she went over the safety rules again until she was sure that Amy understood them. Even more important, she reviewed her own behavior. In the future, she would have to think of safety ahead of any other activity.

They returned home under the watchful eye of Kevin and after lunch, they sat down in the family room with Lucy to sort out their school schedule.

The family room was yet another surprise. It was across the hall from the kitchen and as modern as the other rooms were dated. Here, a sturdy chesterfield and armchairs were set around a fieldstone fireplace with a long wooden mantel. There was a television, VCR, a Ping-Pong table, and lots of floor space, as well as a good-sized table with comfortable chairs around it and smaller tables with two chairs just the right size for children's games.

Ross had explained, the night before, that this room was for *serious* living. This was where the children could play to their hearts' content. They were allowed to bring snacks and drinks into the room, and could leave a game out on a card table if it was not finished.

Lucy sat with the children at one end of the table and discussed with them how they should organize their time and what schoolwork they felt they should do. Lucy was interested to see just what they would say.

The children surprised her. They were both adamant that they wanted to write. It seemed that they were writing their own stories at school. They wanted some time to read, their own choice, they specified. Each child produced a book they were reading. They wanted to go to the science center and museum instead of studying science and history at home. They agreed to try to do something related to arithmetic each day. Robbie was quick to bring out a game with geometric shapes and also to show her games that were on the computer that sat in the corner.

Together, they drew up a schedule that allowed for an hour and a half each weekday for them to read and write. It was understood that the period could be extended if they so wished. Lucy blocked out time to go on at least one of the field trips the children had suggested and left time for some more. They decided when they would skate and when they would do gymnastics. By the end of their planning, the calendar Lucy had made was quite full.

It was then that Ross joined them. "Busy schedule," he remarked as he checked it over. At the same time, he removed his jacket and loosened his tie. With his jacket off, Lucy could not help but notice his fitness. Lean muscles flexed beneath the crisp white shirt. Knife-sharp creases on superbly tailored trousers stressed the length of his legs. A tantalizing waft of after-shave reminded her of the night she had held him so firmly in her arms and tried to dislodge the food stuck in his throat.

"There are a few things that we need to add," he said as he leaned past Lucy and pointed a long finger on the chart. "Saturday we will go for our Christmas tree. Sunday night we'll decorate it." He paused and ran his finger along the squares indicating the days. "Let's see what's missing. Oh, yes, tomorrow you have to practice your parts in the Christmas pageant so that you will be ready to perform on Sunday morning."

Turning to Lucy, he explained, "Every year the children at our church take part in acting out the Christmas story. Rehearsal is tomorrow night at the church. Kevin will take you over and I will pick you all up. It's only a few blocks away from here."

Still looking over the days until Christmas, he added, "Of course, there is the annual Christmas party for the executives, their families, and their office staff. It's held here next Friday. The children will attend and I would be grateful if you would, also, Lucy."

What could she say? It was her job to guard the children. But going to any party created problems. She had only one very basic wool knit dress, quite out of style and quite worn out. She wondered if she could negotiate an advance in pay.

Ross glanced at his watch and then at Lucy. "Do you think they could be excused so they could play outside in the snow before we spoil it by flooding it tonight?"

Again, what could she do but agree? When she got up to go with the children, Ross detained her. "They are safe enough in the backyard since the property is fenced down in the ravine, and it's under surveillance. Anyway, my father wants some fresh air and I like him to spend some time with the children whenever he feels up to it."

He pulled her chair out at the table again. "Sit down, Lucy." She did and found herself at right angles to him, and just a little too close for her liking. "How did it go today?"

In spite of herself, she found herself confessing, "I had a bit of a scare this morning." She could see him snap to attention at that. "There were a few minutes when I thought I had lost Amy. We were trying on clothes. She was finished ahead of me and left the cubicle before I did. When I came out, she was nowhere to be seen." Lucy shuddered as she remembered her panic. "I finally found her a number of aisles over selecting an ear-warmer for her grandfather."

"What would you have done if you hadn't found her right away?"

"I would have gone to the store manager and

asked that they close the doors until she was located.''

He nodded. ''I guess that is as good as anything I would have done. Maybe we should have someone come on your shopping sprees with the three of you.''

Lucy took that as deserved criticism. ''I know I was careless. It won't happen again. One fright like that was enough. And I went over the safety rules with Amy again.''

He watched her through hooded eyes for a moment. ''Lucy. That was not a criticism. I know just how fast Amy can move. She has given me more than a few moments of concern over the years. You will have to take the children shopping again. They will want to buy their Christmas presents. That's something we also have to add to the calendar of events you've so nicely organized.''

When she still found it impossible to hide the sense that she had somehow failed in her job, he went on. ''You can't be expected to have eyes in the back of your head. I'll speak to Kevin. Before you go out, tell him what you intend to do with the children. Let him decide whether he needs to go with you, or follow you at a distance. That's his area of expertise. Make use of it.''

When Lucy would have gotten up to leave, he touched her arm to restrain her movement. Lucy sighed. She couldn't help herself. She found Ross just a little overpowering. How was it that he could just sit by her and all she could think about was him instead of the subjects they were discussing? He seemed to invade her space so that she had a screaming need to sit at the other end of the table.

He hemmed and hawed for a moment while she stewed, then gave her one of his most mellow, green-eyed glances. "Lucy. I have another favor to ask of you."

What on earth could he want? she wondered. Her mind raced over the day's events. Was there something else she should have done?

"I would like you to be my hostess at my staff's Christmas party here in the great entrance."

"Hostess?" she found herself repeating foolishly.

"You would help me greet my guests, make pleasant conversation with one and all, and generally be by my side except when and if the children should need you."

Be by his side? What exactly does that mean? she thought wildly. The hall would be full of beautifully dressed men and women. She had a bizarre image of herself by his side, elegantly clad in running shoes, leotard, and sloppy old leg warmers.

As if reading her mind, he continued, "You will, of course, need a budget to cover the cost of a suitable outfit for the evening. I certainly don't expect you to spend your money dressing up for these occasions. I've asked my father to take you shopping next week. He knows the best places in town for the clothes you'll need.''

"But why me?" she blurted out. "You must know a dozen glamorous women who would act as your hostess. They must be lined up in rows outside your office door.''

"In rows?" he asked with a raised eyebrow. "Outside my office door? Hardly." Then, more seriously, he asked, "Why you? Well, let's say I feel safe with you around. I know you'll come to my rescue should anything unforeseen happen to me.''

He stood up and grinned down at her some more. She was beginning to get suspicious of that disarming grin. He used it when he wanted something. "Actually, one of the reasons I want you to assist me is that I think it's possible you might pick up some clues about the writer of the notes as you circulate among the guests. I still haven't an inkling who is making the threats.''

That made sense to Lucy. Often, an outsider could pick up nuances in situations. However, Ross's next words rattled her completely. "There is another reason, Lucy. I like you, and if you are my hostess, I'll get a chance to dance with you.''

With another saucy grin, he left her sitting at the table, her mouth hanging open with astonishment. Now what on earth did he mean by that mouthful? Surely he was teasing.

That evening, she found another interesting thing

about the Urquhart children. They had jobs. At supper, they helped clean the dishes off the table and put them in the dishwasher. Ross explained to Lucy, ''The children need money for their Christmas gifts and other small needs throughout the year. Therefore, I decided long ago that they would earn the cash they needed. Another of the things they have to do is keep their bedrooms tidy. That's to save Helen's legs. We keep the jobs simple. They make the bed to the best of their ability. They clean up their activities when they are finished. They also bring down their laundry to the laundry room each day. That saves Helen a trip. They must always put everyone's dishes in the dishwasher, regardless of the meal.''

When the children had gone to bed, Lucy thought she would watch some television but when she returned to the family room, she found Ross waiting for her. ''I'd like to show you how the water system works so you can flood the rink throughout the day when you think it needs it. Put on some warm clothes and I'll meet you back here in five minutes.''

So much for resting, thought Lucy wryly. It sounded like she might actually be watering the rink herself.

In the end, flooding the rink proved to be a pleasant pastime. For once, she felt at ease with Ross. It was as if he had banked down that energy field she felt whenever she was near him. Each with a shovel, they flattened and smoothed down the central area of the yard. Together, they took turns hosing the smoothed snow until an even surface appeared.

They didn't say much to each other. Instead, they watched the graceful arc of water, guessed at the stars pulsing at them in the cold, crisp night air, and shared the odd reminiscence about wintertime. When they had finished, Ross thanked Lucy for giving up her spare time to keep him company, and then went off to work in his study.

Lucy, herself, was tired out. Just the stress of having a new job, being in new surroundings, and handling the likes of Ross Urquhart was enough to send her to bed early.

The next morning the children entertained her with the stories they were writing and illustrating. Robbie's was a long, involved one about a boy who wanted to be a hockey goalie. Amy surprised Lucy with the first few pages of a pop-up story. She had cut and glued a character in between the pages of the book so that each time a page was opened, a character stood up. Amy confessed that Robbie had helped her figure out how to do this. Her pages only had a line or so of printing and her illustrations required lots of coloring.

As they worked, Lucy studied the children. There was little of Ross in their faces. Both children had bright red hair, vibrant blue eyes, and delightful ginger freckles. Small snub noses and wide grins added to their charm. Lucy suspected they looked like their mother. They worked together well, although Lucy sensed that was because they were on their best behavior. After a day or so, they would probably bicker the way brothers and sisters often did.

It was still very cold outside but after lunch, they went down to check the ice. Lucy was pleased to discover that Ross's father had flooded the rink again that morning and now it had a very smooth surface.

The harmony of the morning was broken when each child wanted to do something different on the ice. Robbie was all for charging up and down the ice with the hockey stick and puck, while Amy wanted to try figure skating on the fresh, smooth surface, as she had seen on television. In the end, Lucy had to lay down the law by deciding herself the order of their activities, since compromise seemed out of reach. Consequently, a rather disgruntled Robbie was learning to skate backward with Lucy and Amy when Ross appeared by the rink. After watching them for a few minutes, he beckoned to Lucy. Since she had decided the lesson had gone on for long enough, she suggested that Amy learn some hockey from Robbie to keep things fair and left them to it while she skated over to Ross. She couldn't resist doing a fancy spin and coming up sharply with a spray of ice. Instead of smiling at her blatant showing off, he signaled with his head for her to follow him back into the basement out of earshot of the children.

When they were well away from the children, he turned. With a grimace, he ran his fingers through his mane of fair hair. *He's tired,* she thought. Dark shadows of exhaustion she hadn't noticed before ran under his eyes. "We received another note today. It said something about restraining new business ventures or facing the consequences."

Lucy's eyes flew to him in alarm. "What consequences?"

"I wish I knew. Only a few of my top executives and assistants know about the threats. We had a conference today, and for the life of us, not one of us can think what the note is referring to. There is one very important event in the offing but is so secret that I can't imagine anyone knowing about it. Only my most trusted executives know of it. On the other hand, it would not take much to start a rumor that could affect the market whether it was based on truth or not."

"Do you think that could happen?" asked Lucy.

"I don't know. Until today, the threats were directed more specifically toward me rather than the company. It could be because we are taking more precautions, and the children are safely out of sight, that the man or woman who is doing this is getting a little more frantic, and trying to stir up a reaction.''

With a shrug, he dismissed the problem and asked, ''How's the rink?''

Lucy could not help but grin. ''It's great, although there was some discussion over whose activities we would stress first, Robbie's or Amy's. I felt it was time to make it clear just who the boss was, so I decided. Since then, they seemed to have had a good time.''

Ross returned to the rink and watched the children for a few minutes. Lucy had to smile when Robbie called, ''Watch me skate backward.'' As he twisted from side to side and sliced his way backward across the rink, he called, ''Lucy's going to show me how to turn sharply next.''

Ross turned toward the basement. ''I've got to go, Lucy. I'll pick up you and the children from the rehearsal tonight. Keep your eyes open on the way over to the church.'' With a worried frown he bounded up the stairs, leaving Lucy to return to the ice.

Before he left, Ross went to his study window and watched the three figures below. Lucy and Amy were playing against Robbie when suddenly, Lucy went down on her bottom. For a moment, the children stood nervously by her. Lucy lay back on the ice and broke into a peal of laughter. Relieved, they piled on top of her and giggled.

She'd won their hearts whether she realized it or not, he thought. Now, could *he* win her heart?

The pageant practice was a new experience for Lucy. She had never attended church, not even as a youngster, so she was somewhat hesitant about the rehearsal. She need not have worried. The children knew where to go and introduced her politely to the lady in charge.

Lucy was put to work by some enthusiastic mothers who had spent hours making the costumes. They soon had her applying makeup on the various characters and animals that featured in the story.

It turned out that Robbie was to be one of the camels and Amy, one of the lambs. When every child was in their appropriate costume, the rehearsal began. Lucy was charmed. The camel outfits were really brown jackets with a large hump sewn in the back and a hood with ears fitted tightly around each child's face. When the children walked along in them, they swayed from side to side beside the three magi bearing gifts. There was much giggling from a mother and father who had been chosen as two of the wise men.

While they moved through the stages of the presentation, Lucy had time to look around. The rehearsal was in the church hall. Others were setting up scenery and preparing decorations. Her eye was caught by several young people running around doing odd jobs. A particularly handsome man in his early twenties had two pretty young women giving him a hand with the lights on a Christmas tree. There seemed to be as much flirting going on as there was work.

Ross showed up just as the rehearsal was finished. "Come and meet Robbie's hockey coach, just in case you have to take Robbie to practice some morning."

"Morning?" queried Lucy.

"Sure, morning. The kids practice Saturday mornings at eight o'clock at the local community center."

"You mean you get up and take Robbie every Saturday morning?"

"Wouldn't miss it. And Amy is starting after Christmas in the midget league. You must know everything there is to know about early morning practices, Lucy. Your dad would have taken you to many of them."

Lucy thought back to her childhood. Her father certainly had, especially during those years around the time of the Olympics. Now, she wondered how he had managed it. His own job as an independent computer programmer had been tiring enough without extending his hours for rehearsals. Again, she thought of the letter she should write to him. Would it be too late for one to reach her father by Christmas?

Ross took her arm and led her over to the young Casanova and his smitten companions. He really was a good-looking fellow, tall, with short, straight blond hair, very blue eyes, and a charming smile.

Ross introduced Lucy to all three of them, and then said, "Greg, this is Lucy Allen. She is staying with us for a while."

Greg took her hand in a firm grip. "Welcome, Lucy. I noticed they had you working. Be careful. There's always a job waiting for someone around here."

"Greg is Robbie's hockey coach," explained Ross. "Lucy wants to learn how to play hockey so she can take on Robbie and me."

Greg looked at her with renewed interest. "Come out to practice any time you want. I'm sure you'd pick up some points."

As Ross led her away, he told her a little more about Greg. "He's quite a quiz kid. One of those young guys who soaked up computing on their own. He's in business for himself, and, I understand, very much in demand. I know he was contracted by one of our companies."

Lucy looked over her shoulder at the group around the Christmas tree. It was obvious they were enjoying themselves. Laughter and the sound of horseplay followed them across the room. Christmas, thought Lucy, certainly created lots of opportunities for having fun.

She switched her attention back to what Ross was saying. "Young Greg grew up in a public housing complex near here. I understand he was raised by his mother, alone. I have nothing but admiration at the way he has succeeded on his own merits. I know his mother must be very proud of him."

It was seven o'clock when they left the rehearsal. When the group of them went out to the limousine, Lucy was surprised to discover Helen and their grandfather already in the backseat. When everyone was settled, Ross said casually, "I don't suppose anyone would like to go to The Organ Grinder?" The children were ecstatic. "Yes, Daddy. Please, please," Robbie shouted while Amy wound her arms around her father and said, "I want to sit near the organ."

Lucy glanced over at their grandfather, and he smiled at her and rolled his eyes. "I hope you like pizza and organ music. Because, tonight, I fear you are going to get them in abundance."

In no time at all, the group of them, including Kevin, were installed at a round table in a restaurant boasting a pipe organ among its many other charms, and they were all happily digging into the pasta of their choice. When they left, Lucy was surprised to see the waiter hand another heavily wrapped pizza to Helen. "That's for the poor fellows who kept an eye on the limo to make sure no one tinkered with it while we were inside," explained Ross.

As they rode back to Rosedale, Lucy wondered at the wealth that could afford to take a party of seven to a restaurant like that without a qualm. She recalled that one of the biggest treats in her childhood had been the sharing of a pizza with her dad. And that had been only on special occasions.

Lucy helped Helen get the children ready for bed while contemplating a nice quiet soak in her mammoth tub, when Ross found her. "I have some things to show you, Lucy, if you have a moment."

She tried very hard to appear keen instead of long-suffering, and with a glance at her bedroom door, followed her lord and master, as she whimsically called him, to the great entrance.

There, however, her sense of long-suffering was lost in surprise. Spread out in the center of the hall over the pristine black-and-white tiles were four thick gymnastic mats. In the corner, more were piled. There were also several very low balance beams and a mini-trampoline.

"Wow," was all Lucy could say. She walked around and kicked the mats with approval. She tried the balance beams. "When did these arrive?"

"While we had supper." Ross was obviously very pleased with himself, for he walked around, hands in his pocket, and examined each new purchase.

Casually, he asked, "What do you plan to do now?"

Lucy was about to tell him about her date with the bathtub but something about the way he asked the question made her stop. With a shrug, she replied, "Nothing in particular."

"Good," beamed Ross. "Then, you can teach me some tae kwon do for self-defense."

Expecting to hear him say *gymnastics,* she was startled. Teach him tae kwon do? He had to be kidding. But one glance at his interested face was enough to convince Lucy that he was dead serious.

Why couldn't he want to learn gymnastics? She'd gladly teach him to walk the balance beam or bounce on the semi-trampoline. But tae kwon do!

"Is there anything wrong, Lucy?" he inquired.

"Well," she prevaricated, "I wonder just how limber you are?"

"Quite limber, Lucy." He proceeded to bend forward in his well-cut business suit and nearly touch the floor with his fingertips. "When I'm out of this suit, I'm even more limber."

That's what I'm afraid of, she thought. *Preserve me from Ross Urquhart in singlet and shorts. I just couldn't stand it!*

Ross walked to the corner of the hall and pulled a parcel from behind an honest-to-goodness suit of armor. With all the showmanship of a Houdini, he pulled out a white outfit and black belt, and with a bow, presented it to her. "For you, Mademoiselle."

He reached into the bag again and pulled out a similar white outfit for himself.

With smug assurance and the devil's own twinkle in his eye, he watched Lucy as she struggled to find an excuse for not cooperating. ''I suggest that we go to our various rooms and change. Then you can begin your instruction. I want to learn how to disarm someone as neatly as you did the other night.''

Wisely, Lucy decided to save her arguments for later. While she changed into white trousers and a jacket that crossed in front and was held by her black belt, she thought frantically about the procedures she would follow. She knew what she did not want to do. She did not want to do two-person warm-ups. *But,* she thought with a devious smile, *I'm sure that I can wear him out doing one-person exercises.*

When Lucy returned to the entrance hall, she found that Ross had placed the mats to make a large square, and was standing at their side, simply clad in his white trousers and jacket, attentive, deceptively docile, and drop-dead gorgeous.

She invited him to stand at one end of the mats while she stood at the other. A good space, she found to her relief, for Ross was radiating sufficient enthusiasm and male energy to power a nuclear station.

With a straight face, she kept him at the end of the mat, suitably humble as befitted a mere student, and lectured him on the tenets of tae kwon do. "Students must follow a code of rules when they relate to other tae kwon do students and teachers," she announced. "These rules help students follow the central tenets of tae kwon do: justice, respect, loyalty, courtesy, and perseverance."

She then showed him the appropriate way to bow and explained whom to bow to. She carefully avoided telling him that a member of tae kwon do should always obey and respect a person five years older than oneself. This piece of news she was sure he would be sure to exploit at her expense.

When she had lectured long enough to see that he was getting just a little impatient, she moved on to the warm-up exercises. She started with the Hurdler's Stretch, the Front Split, and the Lotus Knee Press. To her surprise, Ross was almost limber enough to handle these exercises with ease. She continued with the Back Arch, the Body Rock, and the Knee Twist, and then declared that that was enough.

To her surprise, Ross did not argue. Instead, he walked to the suit of armor again, and found a book in the bag. Seriously, as if he had no suspicion that she had tried to limit his training, he earnestly asked her if she could teach him some two-person exercises. "Here, look at these," he urged. "I think these exercises would help me achieve the stretch I was unable to reach by myself."

Grinding her teeth, and trying to concentrate her mind on the exercises instead of the superb male body in front of her, Lucy taught him the Two-Person Side Split. But she was sorely tried because Ross insisted on trying each face-to-face stretch. Not satisfied with that, he insisted they try the Body Fold, an exercise where the two partners sat back to back with their legs straight ahead and their arms looped through each other's. The folding proved just a little too much for Lucy, for it brought her just a little too close to Ross. When they finished, she begged time for a rest.

Ross bowed his way off the mat and opened the book again. "Teach me one kick before we stop." When she looked mulish, he coaxed, "C'mon, Lucy. You never know when I might need it. It could save my life."

With a silent prayer for patience, she worked at teaching him the Side Kick. Ross had superb balance. He watched her only once and made an excellent imitation of her kick. At least she could instruct the kick without having to touch him, so she gave suggestions and he practiced. She might have known he could move with the grace of a dancer, something unexpected for such a big man. Lucy could not help but admire the poised extension of his leg as it thrust out into the kick.

Finally, he was satisfied, and insisted that she share a hot chocolate with him before she went off to bed. As she walked ahead of him down the hall to the kitchen, he smiled to himself. The idea of tae kwon do lessons was brilliant, he thought without repentance. He knew Lucy did not like giving them. He knew that she was uncomfortable when they touched and that she worked hard at keeping him at an emotional distance. But he intended to break down her resistance. How better to get to know each other than to work at the exercises? How better to discover whether she really did have those qualities of loyalty, respect, courtesy, justice, and perseverance—qualities that he valued in a mate?

Lucy was deep in a dream where Ross Urquhart was kicking knives out of attackers' hands. Each time he struck, a bell rang. Finally waking, she realized that the telephone beside her bed was ringing.

Lucy reached out and grabbed the receiver. Before she could mumble hello, a voice shattered her eardrums. "Lucy, it's Ross. C'mon. Wake up."

Lucy squinted through the dark at the clock. It was only seven o'clock, and she wasn't even sure whether that was evening or morning. Closing her eyes for a moment, she thought frantically. It had to be morning because they had worked until almost eleven the previous night. Didn't the man ever sleep?

"Lucy!"

Scowling at the receiver, Lucy snarled, "It's only

seven o'clock. There are no lessons until nine o'clock. We agreed.''

''Gee, you're a barrel of fun in the morning, Lucy.''

Lucy refused to acknowledge the sarcasm.

''If you want to see Robbie play hockey, you have to leave in half an hour. I'll see you in fifteen minutes in the kitchen. The coffee's on. Both kids are ready. Wear something warm.''

Before Lucy could get her mouth open, he hung up. What an aggravating man he was. There was no reason on earth why she should get up and go to hockey practice. Lucy turned over and tried to sleep only to find herself well and truly awake. *Nuts,* she thought. *I might as well go.* But there were going to be some rules set. Enough was enough!

Lucy ignored them all as she sipped her coffee. She pretended to be asleep in the car as it made its way to the rink, and she refused to talk to Ross until the children were on the ice. It wasn't that she was trying to be miserable. It was just that she felt foul when she was wakened suddenly and expected to leap about.

As they settled down against the boards of the rink to watch the game, she explained this to Ross in a calm, level voice. ''If you want me to do something early in the morning, all you have to do is tell me the night before so that I can set my clock a half hour earlier. Then, I'll be able to function civilly.''

She waited to see if he understood. Ross grinned. That really annoyed her. There had been enough grinning the night before. ''I'm not amused, Ross,'' she said, and moved down the rink away from him.

Ross watched her go, and laughed. Oh, not so she would hear him, but his shoulders shook with it. His Lucy had a real, honest-to-goodness flaw. She was not Miss Perfection. There was something she could not do. She could not leap out of bed and be civil.

Ross hurried off and purchased another cup of coffee for her. Approaching her carefully, he held out the coffee and said, ''I apologize. I should have asked you last night. I just decided on the spur of the moment that you might enjoy watching the kids play.''

Lucy accepted the coffee graciously and turned to watch the game again. It really was amusing. Robbie was barely eight, and although tall for his age, he still had to pump like mad to move up and down the rink. Boys even a few months older than he was seemed to have an edge in speed and timing. But they all had one thing in common. They were continually getting their feet out of coordination, the hockey stick in their way, and missing the puck. Frequently they hit the puck toward their own goal.

At first Lucy thought she must be imagining it,

but when Ross burst into laughter as the puck shot off in the exact opposite direction it was intended, she had to burst out laughing too.

"Now you know why I thought you would enjoy this." Ross chuckled. "I promise you that they will improve quite quickly. Greg's a good coach."

At this point Greg appeared on the ice and stopped the action. He called the boys into the benches and had a quiet discussion with them. Amy, who had been watching silently until now, turned to Lucy. "Greg always lets the boys play for a few minutes so they can realize what they need to learn. Then he teaches them a lesson."

And that was exactly what Greg did. After a series of skill-development exercises, the boys played a short game. This time, they were much more in charge. Both sides shot in goals.

When the game was over, Ross turned to Lucy. "Are you sorry you came?"

Lucy looked at Ross. She expected to see his usual smug grin and was already forming a smart-aleck reply. But there was no such expression on his face. He appeared quite serious, anxious even. Lucy found herself smiling. "Of course, I enjoyed the game. I'm glad you asked me." He rewarded her with a blockbuster smile, so genuine and different from the grin that she was quite floored. She was touched that her approval should mean so much.

It was decided that they would go for the Christmas tree at one o'clock that afternoon and that Lucy should be undisturbed until lunch. Grateful for the time to herself, Lucy headed back to her bedroom, and over to the elegant desk that sat before one of the windows looking down onto the rink and over the ravine. Searching through its drawers she found pens, pencils, and fine-quality writing paper.

Sitting down, she picked up the pen and began, *Dear Dad . . .*

Ross was working in the library when someone tapped on the door. Glancing at his watch, he saw that it was almost time for lunch. Stretching back from the desk, he called, ''Come in,'' and was surprised to see Lucy enter, some sheets of paper in her hand.

The irreverent thought crossed his mind that she might have drawn up a schedule of times he could wake her, but then he looked at her again and realized by her serious expression that whatever she had come about was more than timetables.

''What can I do for you, Lucy?''

Lucy fiddled with the sheets of paper in her hand for a moment, and then asked, ''Is it possible to send a fax on that machine to Australia?''

''Certainly, Lucy. You can do it right now. Although I'm not sure what time it is in Australia, but

I don't suppose it matters; many places leave their machines on at night. We'll soon know.''

Ross held out his hand for the papers. ''What's the name and number, Lucy?''

Lucy stared at him out of her big gray eyes, the line of dark blue around them even more pronounced. Finally, she cleared her throat and said, almost defensively, ''Ronald Allen,'' and handed him a sheet with the name and number. ''I've decided it's time I tried to make contact with my dad again. That's if he wants to. I thought that if I faxed this letter, it would give him time to write before Christmas if he wanted to.''

As Ross set up the paper and dialed the number, he could not help but hear the loneliness in her voice. He realized, suddenly, that he had not yet settled Christmas with Lucy. Somewhere in the back of his mind, he realized that he had been assuming she would spend the holiday with them. But he certainly had not specified this.

When the fax was received, he returned the letter. ''I was going to come and find you, Lucy. I wanted to discuss this afternoon.''

When she looked mildly confused, he explained, ''The trip to the Christmas tree farm. I'm determined that nothing is going to spoil what has become a special Christmas custom for us. However, I *am* concerned about safety.

''In an effort to make our movements less obvious, I've rented a van for the occasion. One can see out of it well, and also, it's a handy vehicle to have when you want to put a large tree on it.''

''Where do you go to get the tree?'' Lucy asked.

Ross drew Lucy over to a large road map he had on his desk. Pointing to a spot on the map, he went on, ''We have to drive for about an hour up into farming country north of the city. We always go to the same place. It's very busy, full of families making their selection. For that reason alone, it should be fairly safe.

''I'd like you to undertake to keep Robbie with you at all times. I'm going to suggest to him that it is his responsibility to keep you safe, so don't be surprised if he sticks to you like glue.''

Lucy smiled at this. She knew already that Robbie had a very protective streak toward his sister. She could easily imagine him extending it to her.

''How about the guards? Will they be with us?''

''The guards will be in different cars, but will always have us in sight on the road, and someone will be on foot at the farm.''

Lucy turned as if to leave, when Ross cleared his throat. ''Er, Lucy, I realized that I have been assuming something that I may have no right to assume. When I hired you, I assumed that you would spend Christmas Eve and Christmas Day with us. I don't think the danger will be over by then, and with all the things happening, people dropping in and so on, it would really make me feel that the children were safe if you were here. However, if you have other plans you can't change, I'll understand.''

Lucy was embarrassed. She really hadn't thought about Christmas. She had spent it alone more than once since her father had left. It wasn't easy to do but she had succeeded reasonably well. Now, she realized that, deep in her heart, she had been counting on spending the holiday with this man and his family. With as much dignity as she could muster, Lucy replied, ''I am sure I can arrange to stay over Christmas if that is what you want.''

Ross's green eyes glowed emerald with satisfaction. ''I'm quite sure, Lucy.''

As they spilled out of the van, and tramped the trails along with groups of other like-minded families, Lucy felt as if she had been placed on one of those shiny winter photographs that often graced Christmas cards. The sky was a clear, pure blue against which the blackened tree branches glowed golden in the sunlight. Evergreens, rich green against the dazzling snow that had fallen intermittently over the past few days, drooped under its weight. As they passed the rows of trees, small storms of snow dusted from the branches to drift across their laughing faces.

Ross had Amy on his shoulders while Robbie kept a tight grip on Lucy's hand. The feel of his

warm little paw in hers made her glow with an unexpected surge of happiness, and she gave herself
to the activity completely.

They had to walk quite a distance to the bigger
trees. "Because of the age of the house, the rooms
have very high ceilings. It means," Ross explained,
"we put up a tall, full tree. I'm looking for one
between eight and nine feet."

"Not meters?" Lucy teased.

"You and my children may think in meters, but
I am just old enough to have learned yards and
inches. When it comes to short distances, I still
think in inches, feet, and yards," replied Ross.

When they finally found the tree of their choice,
they had to cut it down. "It seems a pity," remarked Lucy.

"I know," said Ross with a sigh. "But as you
can see, they have a very rigorous replanting system
at work. We always recycle our tree by putting it
out by the rink and using it as a bird feeder until
spring. We pour grain over it each day, and the birds
are safe to feed within the protection of its branches.
You can sit in the family room and enjoy the car-
dinals, nuthatches, and chickadees all winter."

Dragging the downed tree along through the
snow was no easy task. Both Lucy and Ross were
working hard with assistance from the two children
when suddenly, Robbie darted off. Dropping her
side of the tree, Lucy turned to chase him when a

voice rang out, "Hi, Robbie. Imagine meeting you here." She was relieved to see the hockey coach and one of the girls from the church coming their way, dragging a tree behind them.

The pair of young people with their rosy cheeks and brightly colored winter clothing made an attractive picture. They were puffing as hard as Ross and Lucy as they passed.

Of course, they had to stop and admire one another's tree. "Jane asked me to help her get a tree for her parents and put it on her car," the young man explained. "She's heading north to Mount Albert when we have it tied down."

They were just about to part when Greg remarked, "I meant to mention how well Robbie was skating. Especially backward. I understand that you are responsible for this, Ms. Allen. I'd be interested in watching you instruct Robbie. Possibly I could pick up some good teaching techniques."

Before Lucy could respond, Ross answered, "Give us a ring when you think you are free to come over. We'll try to set up a time when I'm free too. That way, we can have a bit of a game when you have finished."

As the young people waved good-bye, Lucy wondered to herself just why Ross had to involve himself in any activity she was doing. First it was tae kwon do, now it was hockey. As they moved on down the trail, Lucy chuckled. "I bet he breaks a few hearts."

"Well," Ross observed, "the girls certainly seem to enjoy letting him do it."

Lucy reacted to the chauvinistic remark just as he assumed she would, and they ended up stopping for a snowball fight, much to the children's delight. By the time they made it to the cars, there was no sign of either young person but Lucy was still muttering to herself, "Girls enjoy letting him break their hearts. Such nonsense."

They continued bickering about it while they tied the tree to the racks on the top of the van. When it was secure, they settled back into the van for the trip home. About halfway back, just before they reached the expressway that led south into the city, they found a Tim Horton's and stopped for dough-nuts and hot drinks. By the time they were on the highway, the sun was getting low on the horizon.

Long shadows cut across the roads, blueing the snowbanks and freezing the moisture on the pave-ment. For a long time, the children kept track of the kinds of cars that passed them but as they reached the parkway that led into the downtown area and Rosedale, the children grew quiet. Looking over her shoulder, Lucy saw that they had fallen asleep.

For a few more moments, she held out, then felt her eyelids grow heavy in spite of her efforts to stay awake. Finally, she gave up the struggle, closed her eyes, and let her head fall back on the headrest.

Her head never made it, for as her eyes shut, the van bucked, brakes screamed, and the vehicle spun violently. There was a tearing of metal and Lucy felt herself thrown against the seat belt as the motion stopped. Lucy opened her eyes to discover she was looking back up the parkway at a sea of automobile lights. By some miraculous luck, the traffic had either missed them as they spun around or managed to stop.

Even as the world stopped veering drunkenly, and the thought of the children was entering her mind, Ross gasped. "The children!" Releasing his seat belt with trembling hands, he began to crawl between the large van seats.

Lucy turned to see the two children safely belted into their seats, looking more confused than hurt. The sight of their frantic father clambering toward them somehow communicated his fear, and Amy began to cry.

As Lucy unclipped her seat belt, a man appeared at the van window. She recognized him as one of the security guards from the house. He tried to open the door. Lucy leaned against the door and with a screech of metal, it finally gave beneath her weight.

"Are you okay? Is Ross? The children?" he demanded.

Lucy turned to see Ross hunkered down between

the children, an arm about each. He nodded his head in answer, but Lucy could see that it was with an effort and that he was trembling.

At that point, a police cruiser, its light flashing, arrived on the other side of the parkway. Within moments, two officers were out of the cruiser and across the two lanes to where the van was leaning into the safety fence in the outside lane.

It was then that Lucy realized just how lucky they were. A few more degrees to the right and the van would have rolled over the fence and down the incline into the ravine below.

The calm voice of the officer ordered, "See if you can put your seat back a bit so that the gentleman can pass the children out."

Lucy did, and was about to get out of the way when the van gave a sickening teeter. Immediately, the officer detained her. "Stay where you are. There does not appear to be any gasoline spilled but your position is more precarious than I thought. Just to be safe, we'll wait until the fire truck arrives."

As he spoke, a fire truck came up the road and was directed beside the van by the officer. Over its siren, Lucy could hear Ross speaking gently to the children, and heard him say to the officer, "Can you open the sliding door?"

"It's jammed, sir. Just wait a moment until we secure the van to the fire truck, then we'll get you all out. Is anyone hurt?"

"The children are fine," Ross said. Turning, he asked, "Lucy?"

"I'm fine."

The firemen secured the van to the fire truck with thick cables, and then the officer said, "You can release the children from their seat belts, sir. You were wise to wait." Then, turning to Lucy, "Here, let me help you out."

A moment later, Lucy was standing beside the van waiting for Amy. Ross had obviously succeeded in calming her, for Amy went quietly into her arms and clung there, her eyes as big as saucers as she looked at the policemen, firemen, and the very large fire truck.

Lucy saw Ross whisper something to Robbie, saw Robbie nod his head, and then Ross handed him out to the policeman. The moment Robbie's feet touched the ground, he went over and stood by Lucy. He gripped the corner of her jacket and waited, as in awe of the fire truck, cruiser, and rescue personnel as Amy.

Finally, Ross was assisted out of the van. It was then, and only then, that Lucy felt herself relax. To her utter horror, she began to tremble. She hugged Amy, and tried to ward off the spasms, but a fireman was too observant. He said something to the officer in charge, who turned and looked at Lucy and the children. Then he came over. "Did you see what happened?"

Lucy fought down the trembling and tried to say in a calm voice, "I was just dozing off and my eyes were closed. The children were already asleep."

The policeman nodded at this information and walked back to where another officer and the fireman were talking to Ross and the guard. They conferred for a moment and the officer returned. "I'm calling for another cruiser. Since neither you or the children saw anything, I think the wisest thing is for us to get you three home. Mr. Urquhart has asked that you call his physician and have him check both you and the children. He said his father would know the number."

Lucy looked over at Ross, and he nodded in agreement. Lucy wanted to assure herself that he was really all right, but could tell that it was not the moment to fuss. Taking Robbie's hand, she followed the officer to await the cruiser.

Before the children could realize they were being separated from their dad, she charmed them with the idea of riding in the police car. When it did arrive, the novelty carried the moment. The young policeman was sport enough to let the siren wail for a minute as they sailed along the parkway toward the Rosedale exit. Both children were thrilled and instead of crying, spent their time asking questions of the officer about radio dispatch.

Lucy hated to startle Robert Urquhart with the news of the accident, but he handled it well, going off to telephone the doctor, who, he assured her, was a close friend and lived nearby.

When the doctor came, Lucy helped him check the children. He suggested they have a nice warm bath in case they had strained against the seat belts, and then an early night. He sent them off with Helen and then turned to Lucy.

Lucy took one look at him and burst into tears. Embarrassed beyond belief, Lucy snuffled into his hanky while he waited patiently. Finally, she calmed herself and he checked her over. Aside from a little soreness from being thrown against the seat belt, she was fine. As the doctor left, he instructed, ''Telephone me when Ross gets in. I'll come back and check him over if he thinks it's necessary.''

Ross called from the police station to tell them he would be held up and to have supper without him. He promised to be home in time to tuck the children in. He also promised to phone the doctor.

Lucy was reading a story to the children in Amy's room when Ross finally showed up at the bedroom door. The minute the children saw him, they were out of bed and in his arms. They were full of questions. Did he have to go to the police station? Did he get a ticket? Where was the van? And more important, where was the Christmas tree?

Ross sat down on the end of Amy's bed and answered their questions. Yes, he had to go to the police station and make a statement. When the children asked what that meant, he explained patiently. The van, it seemed, was to be inspected by the police and then taken off to be repaired. Lucy wondered why the inspection was necessary. In fact, she was dying to know exactly what had happened but made no effort to find out. He explained to the children that he did not get a ticket and the Christmas tree was in the basement warming up so its branches would fall enough for them to decorate it the next day.

Ross tucked the two children into their beds and waited until each had fallen asleep. Lucy went downstairs to the family room ahead of him to wait impatiently for the whole story.

Lucy and Helen were watching television before the fireplace when Ross finally came into the family room. As soon as he had assured Helen he was all right and that he had eaten, she excused herself.

The fireplace cast a warm glow across the room as Ross sat down wearily on the chesterfield. Lucy sat in a big armchair at right angles to him. For a few minutes, Ross sat silently, seeming to gather himself together. Lucy could see him doing it, could see the muscles tense with the effort it took, could see the grimness of his expression and the weariness beneath his eyes. One of his hands kept clenching and unclenching.

Finally, she could stand it no longer. She asked quietly, "What happened, Ross?"

"We were cut off, Lucy. The action was deliberate, probably a spur-of-the-moment decision by whoever it is that wants to harm us. The car pulled out alongside of me without warning, and before the security car could react, cut across against me, clipping my side and causing me to slam on the brakes, start to spin, and finally veer along the side of the guardrail, where we settled."

"What do they know about the car?" Lucy asked.

"Nothing. The light was very poor. The overhead lights were just coming on. It seemed the back bumper of the car was loaded with snow so that it was impossible to see the license or for that matter, much about the make of the car. Like the time on the subway platform, whoever did it acted without fear and almost impulsively. The thing that saved me was the fact that I have very good reflexes and the people behind were very alert and careful drivers."

Lucy shook her head in perplexity. "I don't understand how he could get away so fast."

"He picked his spot, Lucy, just before an exit."

For the longest time, Ross sat silent, his elbows on his knees, his head in his hands. Lucy longed to go over, brush back the thatch of ruffled hair, and offer some sort of comfort.

Finally, he broke the silence. He looked at her, anguish carved on every feature, his eyes dark with misery. "Do you know what is so absolutely terrifying about this?"

When all she could do was shake her head, he rasped, "It's the terrible helplessness of it all. Right now, there doesn't seem to be a thing I can do about this but wait until the lunatic strikes again."

His body shuddered with a sigh. "And the worst thing of all is that I've been through this before." When Lucy looked confused, he explained, "When Natalie took sick, there was not one single thing I could do to make her better. Nothing they tried worked. Neither my wealth nor power could alter the course of her illness. In the end, the disease won, and she died. And I had to sit there and watch it all happen. Just like now."

He sat, his hands over his mouth, and struggled with his demons. Finally, he made as if to ease his anguish by hunching his shoulders. He let out a yelp. With a wry expression, he rubbed his neck and shoulder. "I don't suppose you took massage as part of your training? I must have wrenched my shoulder trying to keep the van on the road."

Lucy's heart sank. In all honestly, she could help him. But Ross vulnerable and hurting was a powerful assault to her defenses. "Actually, I know quite a lot about massage," she admitted. "You pick it up when you are a gymnast. Come over here and let me examine your shoulder."

Ross got up, came over to Lucy, and knelt before

her chair. When Lucy ran her hands across his shoulders and along the muscles that edged his spine, she was shocked. They were as hard as rock.

"Take your top off, Ross, and lie down on the floor. Facedown." She threw him a small cushion to place his head on, and kneeling beside him, began to work.

She started at his neck, thumbing the muscles close to his skull, stroking the long ones that held his head erect, and then moving on to the muscles of the shoulders and back. It took ages before she began to feel him relax. But after a while, she felt the energy begin to flow back through her fingers and the palms of her hands. The tension began to leave his back, his knotted leg muscles, and rigid neck so that finally, as she quieted her movements, she heard him sigh and felt the last of the resistance leave him.

She let out her own breath slowly, and without thought, reached up, and with the back of her hand, stroked the side of his face. Astonished at her action and the depth of feeling that had stirred her to touch him so, she went to get up but before she could, Ross gripped her wrist, and turning, sat up.

His action had her back on her knees, facing him. "Don't draw away from me, Lucy," he whispered. Gently, he cupped her face with his hands and drew her toward him. "Thank you, Lucy," he breathed as he kissed her forehead, her eyes, and finally, her mouth. ''Thank you for the massage. Thank you for saving my life. Thank you for your generosity of heart and your kindness.''

Again he kissed her. This time Lucy responded. She wound her arms around his neck and gave as generously as she received. It was Ross who finally broke away, but only to draw her to his side as he settled himself against the chesterfield before the fire, pulling her head down on his shoulder and tucking her against him.

As they sat there, watching the flames dance, cool reason returned to Lucy. What on earth was she playing at? She had resolved a long time ago that she was not going to get involved with anyone until she had fulfilled her career plans. And then she was going to have time to see the world. She would not be like her father and have to miss all those interesting experiences because she was tied down. And anyway, she reminded herself, she must be mad to get involved with a man like Ross. He was the stuff heroes were made of. Attractive to a fault, powerful, ambitious, and rich. She could imagine the kind of women he spent his time with. Certainly, they were not thin, tall, ordinary looking gym teachers.

Ross felt her withdrawing and turned her toward him. Cupping her face, he said gently, ''Don't write me off, Lucy.''

The remark startled her. Was that what she had

been doing? How had he known about her reservations?

Ross smiled at her from those green, green eyes that tonight, seemed as dark as shadowed forest waters. "I know we haven't known each other long, but it seems to me that we have lived through several lifetimes, if you count the crises we have shared. I'm attracted to you, Lucy. Have been since you wrapped your arms around me and knocked the wind and that piece of chicken bone out of me."

When Lucy would have stirred, he continued, "I recognized your body when I pulled you into the limousine, do you know that? I remembered the scent of your beautiful hair and the softness of your cheek against my jaw when you did the Heimlich."

Lucy was flustered and tried to pull her face away from his frank gaze. "Give us a chance to become friends, Lucy. Give us a chance to see if this attraction we feel for each other can develop into something lasting." When she made no reply, he added, "Please."

Her eyes flashed up at that. The word was not one of supplication so much as one requesting permission. She considered him for a long moment, trying to sort out her impressions, but all she could see was sincerity and all she could feel was the strong compulsion to be in his arms.

Finally, she smiled. "Okay, Ross. Let's see what happens. But I want you to know that I have strong reservations. I am not sure that I want a serious friendship, let alone a romance, but I would be dishonest if I did not admit that I'm attracted to you.''

With that, he had to be satisfied. He stood and pulled her to her feet. Together they sat down and discussed the accident. They planned the next day's activities. They would decorate the Christmas tree. If Ross could, he would arrange a meeting with the head of the detective agency he had employed to assist in the search for the man or woman who was threatening them. Finally, he would tell the children that they would not be able to attend church tomorrow, or take part in the pageant. Ross wanted to review his security before he let the children outside the house again.

When Lucy struggled into the kitchen the next morning, sore from the accident, and tired from sleeping little and worrying much over her attraction to Ross, she was met by a series of sorrowful faces. Amy was sitting on Ross's knee, her eyes puffy from crying, while Robbie was shoving his food around on his plate with little enthusiasm.

As Lucy went to sit down, Amy burst out, ''We can't take part in the pageant today.'' The biggest tears Lucy had ever seen filled Amy's eyes, and brimmed down her small face. With a hiccup, Amy sobbed, ''Daddy says it's not safe to go out because of the accident.''

Lucy risked a glance at Ross. He looked exhausted and very grim. Lucy smiled at Amy. "Isn't it a good thing, then, that I saw you in it the other day? In fact, seeing the rehearsal rather than the real pageant was more fun, Amy. I got a chance to see parts over and over again as the children practiced. Don't you remember? You had to say your 'Baa-a-a' until you got it right."

In spite of her disappointment, Amy smiled, and made a feeble "Baa-a-a."

Glancing at Robbie, she saw that her ploy had not worked on him. "Freddie Swanson is going to take my part. He'll get to sway like a camel and everything."

In the silence that followed this heartbroken complaint, Lucy could see from Ross's expression that he was running out of reserve. She poured herself some orange juice and then remarked casually, "Do you know that I have never seen a Christmas tree put up, nor have I ever decorated one except once or twice in school when I was allowed to make a decoration for the classroom tree?"

The very idea of such a lack of experience caught the children's imagination. "Didn't your parents buy a tree, Lucy?" Robbie asked.

This was the tricky part. Lucy felt as if she was walking through a mine field of emotion. "My father had to work very hard to pay for all my special gymnastic lessons. There was never any money left over for a tree. He thought it was more important that I have a chance to achieve my dream of being an excellent gymnast.''

"Were you very poor?'' Amy asked. Ross went to say something but Lucy stopped him. She knew why Amy asked the question. They had been reading the Hans Christian Andersen fairy tale *The Little Match Girl* the night before. They had talked about poverty and the way it affected the life of the little match girl. "We weren't poor, Amy. We had lots to eat, a home, and warm clothes. My father had a good business. We just did not have money for extras.''

"Where was your mummy?'' Amy asked.

"My mummy died when I was a baby, so you see, my father had to be both mummy and daddy for me.''

Amy turned her face into her father's shoulder and mumbled, "My mummy died, too.'' Then with a radiant smile, she eased her father's heart. "My daddy has had to be mummy and daddy, too.''

Robbie suddenly perked up. "You can help us put up *our* Christmas tree. Can't she, Daddy?''

Ross stood up. "She sure can, son.'' And looking over Robbie's shoulder at her, he mouthed the words, "Thank you.'' Then, turning toward the corridor that led to the library, he said, "Helen, would you show Lucy where the boxes of decorations are. Maybe Lucy and the children could bring the boxes up while I do some phoning. I shouldn't be more than half an hour.''

The children and Lucy had just completed carrying the boxes into the family room when the intercom rang. Helen answered it and told Lucy that Ross wished to see her in the library for a moment.

As Lucy walked over to the library, she wondered what Ross wanted. With the children so upset over missing the pageant, she had forgotten about the night before. Maybe Ross wanted to pursue this or maybe he was setting up the meetings he had mentioned and needed her assistance.

When Lucy entered the library, Ross rose from his desk and showed her several papers. ''These came in on the fax a few moments ago, Lucy. They have to be from your father since they're from Australia. I didn't read them.''

Lucy could feel the color drain from her face. She could see that at least one of the pages had considerable typing on it. She wondered what her father had to say. A surge of hope at the same time as she feared rejection rocked her. However, waiting only made it worse, so she held out her hand for the papers.

Seeing the turmoil in her face, Ross asked, ''Do you want me to stay?''

Feeling too vulnerable to share her feelings, Lucy shook her head. Taking the sheets of paper, she went over to the window and began to read them as Ross left the library.

"Dear Lucy," she read. *"You cannot know what a wonderful Christmas surprise it was to receive your letter. I cannot tell you how happy it has made me."*

Her father went on to say how much he regretted the way he had said good-bye. He explained that it was because he was so upset that it was necessary to leave her that he had done it so poorly. He realized now that he should have explained more carefully to Lucy that the opportunity he had to develop his business in Australia had been a chance of a lifetime. Lucy sighed. She should have been more understanding and not so ready to feel betrayed.

Her father went on to say that he hoped that she would come out to see him, that he would send her the money for a ticket when she was free to use it. He also mentioned that he had met a very nice woman, Lorraine, of whom he was becoming very fond. She was a widow with a grown son and daughter.

He concluded his letter with the words:

Lucy, we're celebrating Christmas although it seems strange to think of turkey dinners, Santa Claus, and Christmas trees in a countryside bright with flowers. It makes me remember the way I mishandled Christmas. I

*failed you there, too, Lucy. Lorraine has taught
me that. At the time, I thought that since I
could not afford all the wonderful presents I
would like to give you, I would pretend that
Christmas and the joy of giving and receiving
was an illusion. I know now that it is the
thought, not the value of the gift, that counts.
Please forgive me. I hope you have the opportunity to share the joys of Christmas with
friends this year. Please telephone on Christmas Day, collect.*

He finished with his telephone number.

Lucy found that there were tears pouring down
her face. Rubbing her cheeks with the backs of her
hands, she turned to see Ross enter the library. He
took one look at her, came over, and took her into
his arms. "Ah, Lucy, don't cry. I can't bear it. Tell
me what's wrong and I'll try to fix it."

Lucy smiled at his arrogance. "Nothing's wrong.
In fact everything is right. Here, read my letter and
see for yourself." While he read, she stayed, snug-
gled against his chest, enjoying the sense of caring
and security his arm around her created. "You were
right about my father, Ross."

"I never said anything particular about your father," Ross corrected.

"Yes, you did," she argued. "You made enough
remarks to start me thinking. It was because of your

attitude that I wrote. Thanks for your help.'' And with a smile, she kissed him on the cheek and then, quickly, got herself away from the temptation of a real kiss.

The problem with her father might be solved, but she was no nearer deciding how she felt about Ross, or for that matter, the children who were a part of him.

Lucy discovered that erecting and decorating a Christmas tree was no easy task. First, you had to get it placed straight in its holder. It took Ross's long arms and Helen and Lucy's assistance to accomplish this feat. Then, there were the lights. Meters and meters of them as far as Lucy was concerned. Robbie and she stretched them out on the floor, testing each set and groaning loudly when they discovered they had to find a dead light and replace it.

They all laughed when Ross lifted Robbie on his shoulder so that he could begin to drape the strings of lights on the top boughs. Soon the tree was a mass of twinkling fairy lights. Lucy closed the curtains so they could get the full effect and found herself clapping with delight.

Ross forgot his problems for a few moments when he saw Lucy's face. Her eyes were as bright as the myriad of lights on the tree as she explored in the boxes, searching out celluloid animals from an earlier age, delicately laced and beribboned

Victorian baubles, and a set of brightly painted wooden figures.

In the artificial light, her polished chestnut hair swirled about her head with every move. She reached high branches to place a small ornament and moved with such grace that his heart caught in his throat. It was terrifying to think that he could experience such happiness twice in his life but that seemed to be what was happening. He knew, without a doubt, that Lucy was for him. Now, all he had to do was convince her.

Amy opened the last box and rushed over to get Lucy to look at it especially. "This is the family box, Lucy. It has very special ornaments in it." Digging about, she found an angel. "Daddy gave this to Mummy when I was a baby. It goes on the top."

Running over to her father, she handed him the angel. "Lift me up, Daddy, so I can put it on the top."

Lucy watched Ross lift his small daughter up, watched Amy laugh as she placed the angel, and felt a terrible tug at her heart for the woman who was no longer there to share this moment.

The minute Amy was back at the box, she found more treasures. There was a beautiful hand-carved and hand-painted horse that Ross had bought when Robbie was a baby, an exquisite glass angel Ross had given to Natalie, and a cunning old-world nut-cracker Natalie had given to him. She was aware that the family was rejoicing in the mementos. The memory of the lost wife and mother seemed to spark an arc of energy that brought them all great joy, even Lucy.

When the tree was finished, and glowing and twinkling in all its glory, Helen brought in a warm Christmas punch made from cranberries and they all sat around the fire and admired their handiwork.

"Now we have to do our Christmas shopping," Robbie announced. "I have almost all my list made, Daddy." And then, as he sensed his father's disquiet, he asked for reassurance. "We *are* going to be able to go shopping, aren't we?"

"Unless there is another emergency, I don't see why not. I don't think I can go with you, but I am sure Lucy would take you. Kevin can help you also."

"What about Grandma Prentiss?" asked Amy.

"I promise you that we will take over her presents and a tree on Tuesday, which means you had better get busy and get her gifts purchased or made."

For the rest of the afternoon, the children occupied themselves by painting small plaster figures meant for a crèche. These were arranged on the fireplace mantel when they were completed. It was just as they finished that Ross came back to the family room to announce that Greg had telephoned and suggested he and another young woman called

Susie come over and play hockey after supper for a while. Excited by this, there were no more long faces. The children bolted down their food, changed to their skating togs, and went out to clear the ice of any snow that had drifted down.

While they were occupied, Ross explained to Lucy, "I have arranged for Sam Cowan, the investigator who is helping with this case, and Kevin, on behalf of the security crew, to meet with you and me and my personal assistant tomorrow morning about nine-thirty. Do you think that you can arrange to have the children set up with schoolwork so you can attend the meeting? Helen has offered to supervise whatever you have ready for them to do."

Lucy was sure she could have the children working happily at their writing, so she agreed to come to the meeting. Privately, she was delighted that Ross valued her presence there.

Skating that night was great fun. Everyone, including Greg and Susie, practiced inside edges, outside edges, and spinning. There were great hoots of laughter as the men, in particular, wobbled in an attempt to create a graceful spin on the ice. Later, Ross, Robbie, and Lucy took on Greg, Susie, and Amy. Amy's day was made when she actually got a goal. If there was anything slightly wrong with the evening, it was the fact that Lucy felt Greg was very subtly coming on to her. Yet, when she watched the others as Greg occasionally monopolized her, they seemed not to notice. In the end, she decided it must be her imagination. Maybe that was the only way Greg knew how to behave. He certainly had the girls lined up to keep him company. On the other hand, maybe he found safety in numbers.

Ross was always surprising Lucy at the casual way he lived in the sprawling stone mansion. Instead of having the meeting in the library or in one of the other elegant rooms in that wing, he held the meeting around the pine table in the comfy kitchen.

When Lucy slipped in, the men were standing around sipping from coffee mugs and munching on some of Helen's delicious cookies. Kevin was there, a slight, wiry man still in his leather bomber jacket. There was also a younger man in a tailored suit whom Lucy had already met and knew was Ross's PA. Surprisingly, Robert Urquhart was there, looking much better than he had when Lucy had first seen him in the restaurant. Every day, he seemed stronger and more dynamic. Finally, Lucy's attention was drawn to the stranger in the group. He was a tall man, erect in carriage, with graying close-cropped hair and a rugged face. She found him watching her alertly. *Nothing's likely to escape his notice,* Lucy thought.

Ross took her arm and led her over to the stranger. ''Sam, I'd like you to meet Lucy Allen, the children's temporary teacher and bodyguard. She is the young woman who saved my life last week. I told you about her, remember?''

Sam smiled and held out a big paw. ''I understand that you also have a mean kick and are trying to teach Ross here some new tricks.''

Lucy decided it was safest to nod acknowledgement rather than discuss those infamous lessons. Just when she had thought she had succeeded in slipping off to bed last night before Ross remembered his lessons, the bedroom telephone had rung and the summons had gone out. Lessons began in five minutes. This time, Ross had really read the book. Consequently, he had been demanding and thorough, and Lucy had found herself far too closely involved in the instruction and exercises for her peace of mind. Especially as she began to realize that the tae kwon do was very much part of a campaign Ross seemed to have devised to ensure that she was aware of him at all times.

Just as if to confirm her thoughts, Ross took her arm in a proprietary manner and led her over to a chair, then brought her coffee and a cookie. Taking a seat, he began the meeting.

Looking at John, his PA, Ross asked, ''What's the latest on the accident yesterday?''

John placed glasses on a rather scholarly face and flipped open a notepad. ''The car was found that hit your van. As you suspected, it was stolen some time ago. The assailant had nerves of steel, however, or was downright foolhardy, because he must have followed you when you went out yesterday so that he would know where you were on the parkway. The chances were high that the police would spot the car in spite of the fact that it was very dirty and the license was covered up with snow.''

Glancing around to make sure everyone was with him, John continued, ''The police checked the car for fingerprints, etc., and found nothing useful. They think the driver just whipped off down the exit ramp and at the top of the hill turned into Rosedale and headed for one of the ravine parking lots.''

Robert Urquhart looked up alertly at that piece of news. ''That means the driver is familiar with the Rosedale area. As you know, it's almost impossible for a stranger to find his or her way among the crescents and ravines without getting lost the first time.''

''Good point, sir,'' acknowledged Sam. ''Although again, it could be just plain luck.''

Ross turned to Kevin. ''What can you add?''

''Only that the car was noted along with the other cars on the road by the team watching yours. At no time did it attract any unusual attention. When it did strike, it did so with such speed that we were unable to react in time to protect you.'' Kevin wore a wry look of apology as he said this. ''This does not make me any happier than it must you, Ross. We seem to be dealing with someone who simmers along, close by, and then suddenly snaps or acts. It's the complete unexpectedness of the assaults that make them so effective.''

''So we can identify more characteristics of this individual,'' stated Sam. ''He premeditates in that he seems to hover about until an opportunity occurs. That means there may have been times when he was about when he took no action because it was too dangerous.''

''A happy thought,'' interjected Robert Urquhart dryly.

''He also has nerves of steel and reacts very quickly when he does decide to make a move.''

''I suggest,'' said Kevin, ''that we add people to the team whose sole role it is to look for repetitions, for example, the same face in a crowd or the same car on the road. Spotters who are skilled at this and who are not trying to do anything else, drive a car, or act as guard.''

Ross looked at Sam, and Sam nodded in agreement.

''What about taking the children out?'' Lucy asked. ''They are counting on doing their Christmas shopping and they want to visit their grandmother.''

''Grandmother?'' asked Robert with raised eyebrows.

''Mrs. Prentiss, Dad.''

When Lucy looked confused by this, Ross smiled. "I'll explain later."

Turning to the group, Ross said grimly, "I really hate to let this monster get away with what he's doing. I do not want him spoiling Christmas for the children." Looking at Kevin, he said, "I would like to let them go about their activities, if you think you can keep them safe. How about it?"

It was obvious that Kevin was not happy about being put on the spot. "After yesterday, I think it is clear to us all that this person is capable of great daring, so I would be foolish to say there was no risk. However, I think if we use the limo, take an extra driver and watcher in the front so that I am free to sit in the back with Lucy and the children, we could make it to the stores. I'd like to suggest that we avoid places like the Eaton Centre with its crowds and multiple levels. There are lots of smaller malls with at least one department store. For that matter, we could go to The Bay, enter through the hotel next door, and pick up Lucy and the kids from there. We could have extra staff watching in the lobby and others watching them in the store."

"Good idea," agreed Ross. "Let's go for it."

At this point, Sam brought out a sheaf of papers from his briefcase. "I have made copies of the threatening notes Ross received, including one that came this morning. They are numbered. Number one came before he was pushed, number two before the brakes were tampered with. Number three was the threat about the children's safety, four about the company, and five came this morning.''

Sam handed out copies of the papers to each of them. ''I thought it would be useful if we all looked at them to see if they rang any bells. Is there something about the texts that seems familiar? Can you get a sense of the writer's personality?''

For a few minutes, everyone was silent as they read them through. Lucy found them quite fascinating. The others discussed features of the threats while she half listened and read over and over again their wording. The men remarked on the fact that the person had cut the letters out of many kinds of newspapers and magazines, that the spelling was accurate and the message brief. The type of paper used as backing and even the supposition that the letters were cut out with nail scissors occupied their attention.

In addition, Sam informed them that he had a team of experts going over company business, since the only way the person could have been aware of the details referred to must have been through the electronic information available.

At last, they seemed to run out of ideas. Lucy waited, sure that they would notice something that had leaped out at her. When it became clear they had not, she decided to risk their patience and/or derision.

"Umm . . ." She shuffled the papers and waited for their attention. "There is one other thing I noticed. It may be nothing." She hesitated, looking shyly at the rest of them.

"Come on, Lucy," demanded Ross. "If you noticed something, for heaven's sake, tell us."

"Well, I suppose it isn't important, but there seems to be a theme running through them. For example, look at the words used . . . *'restrain, lock up, prisoner be, confine,'* and the last one particularly, *'stay captive in your castle.'* "

Looking up, she saw that they were not exactly impressed. "I studied quite a bit of psychology to get my degree. One of the courses had an entire section studying the way people choose their words, especially if they are mentally ill. Their choice of language is often a clue to their problem." With a shrug, she continued, "I think it would be useful to approach a criminal psychologist, and have him or her evaluate these. It might provide you with more characteristics of the individual or even a clue to his or her motive."

Sam sat back, folded his arms across his chest, and looked at Lucy carefully. Then he said to Ross, "You have a live one here, Ross. She's worth her weight in gold. I should have seen this. It's so obvious. And she's right. With your permission, I'll get these to a specialist we use immediately."

Lucy felt herself blush brightly at his words of

praise. Briefly, she flashed a look at Ross to assess his opinion. She was startled to see that he was directing one of his green-eyed glances with such boldness that, if possible, she blushed even more.

Finally, he released her from the grip of that intense survey and announced, "Lucy's right. But while we are here, let's do a little brainstorming. Does anyone have a clue why these words of confinement seem to be important to our assailant?"

They all took turns at suggesting explanations but none of them worked. Finally, the meeting wound down. They finished by discussing the details necessary to make the Christmas party safe. Ross absolutely refused to consider canceling it. "It's been a company and family tradition since the time of my great-great-grandfather and I refuse to let some crazy stop us."

As the meeting broke up, Ross touched Lucy's arm. "Give me a moment so that I can explain about the children's grandmother."

Lucy tidied up the kitchen for Helen as the men gathered their materials and dispersed. Finally they were gone and only Ross and his father were left. "That was a very astute observation about the wording of the notes," remarked Robert.

Lucy smiled her thanks. "About the children's grandmother?"

"Well, it's this way," explained Ross. "Mrs. Prentiss is a member of the church, a widow with no family and little income. With her permission, the children have adopted her as a grandmother.''

''There's more to it than that,'' continued Robert Urquhart. ''Ross did not like the way the young people in the church suddenly developed consciences at Christmas and spent a lot of time collecting food and gifts, delivering them, and then forgetting about the less fortunate until the next Christmas season. He read somewhere about a program for elderly seniors with no family becoming honorary grandparents. Mrs. Prentiss is their honorary grandmother.''

Ross absentmindedly straightened the chairs from the meeting. Then as if he had come to a decision about something, he said, ''I try to see that the children get to see her at least once every two weeks, more when possible. As you can imagine, it is important that we get to see her several times over Christmas. I plan to take the children to see her and set up a Christmas tree for her tomorrow night. She lives close by in one of the public housing apartments south of Bloor Street.''

''Do they have all the things they need—a tree, decorations, presents?'' asked Lucy.

''Now, there you have the problem. Normally, we would have grabbed a moment here or there to do this shopping, but these threats have taken all my time. I have not wanted to go out without an entourage of guards, which, as you can see, is getting longer and more cumbersome. I wonder if you could sit down with the children today and see what gifts they have in mind for Mrs. Prentiss. They are going to purchase these with their own money. They also may decide to make something for her.''

Lucy was touched to be part of the process. She had had no grandmother. It would be fun to help the children plan and shop for Mrs. Prentiss. It would also be pleasant to be there when they gave her the tree and gifts. ''I'll be glad to help, but I must point out that we are never going to get down to working seriously with all that gymnastic equipment at the rate we are going.''

Ross gave her one of his glintiest green looks and with a smug little smile said, ''Don't worry about it. I am sure there will be time.''

Planning Grandma Prentiss's Christmas turned out to be a learning experience for Lucy. The children seemed to have unlimited enthusiasm. Even Helen was involved. Helen, it seemed, had made boxes of cookies and jars of jam for the lady, who it seemed, had a very sweet tooth.

Robbie told Lucy gravely that Mrs. Prentiss liked to talk about the Royal Family, so he thought he would buy her a book about them. Lucy was amazed at such a thoughtful gift, perfect for one of Mrs. Prentiss's generation.

Amy had decided that she would buy her some

pleasant-smelling bath powder, and put it at the top of her shopping list.

With Lucy's encouragement, they prepared the rest of their shopping list. Lucy was surprised. For such a wealthy family, the children's idea of a suitable gift was very simple and reasonably priced. Robbie had chosen a popular video for his grandfather, while Amy wanted a *Peanuts* comic book for him. "He likes Charlie Brown," she confided. "He always reads the comic strip in the newspaper."

Lucy was suddenly swamped by a wash of emotion. Looking at their serious freckled faces, their sparkling blue eyes, vibrant carroty hair, and enthusiastic smiles as they talked about their list and carefully printed out their needs, Lucy wondered how she would ever bear to leave them.

Getting up, she walked over to the window and stared blindly out at the cold winter scene. Her life and all that she believed in seemed to be splintering out in all directions like light on a Christmas tree ornament. People were elbowing their way into her carefully controlled plans. With a sigh, she returned to the table, and caught a glimpse of the list that Amy was in the act of turning over. To her dismay, she saw her name on it.

What would she do? It had never even crossed her mind to think of gifts. It was not something she was used to doing. Worse still, she had no money.

For that matter, when would she ever get time to shop if she did get some cash? And then, she remembered, her check from the Board of Education should be waiting for her downtown where she had asked them to hold it when she had left her apartment.

Leaving the children for a moment, she approached Helen. "Helen, I know that you have already had to look after the children, but do you think you could entertain them again while I go downtown to collect my paycheck?"

Helen smiled at Lucy. "I was just going to make some Christmas cookies. I always like to have some in when the young people come caroling. The children can help me." Then as Lucy went to leave, Helen added, "You will phone Ross and tell him you are planning to go out? Kevin drove him to work and I'm not quite sure who is on transportation."

It was at that moment that Lucy began to understand just how cornered Ross must feel. Never had she had to stop and think about the safety of her own actions, except, of course, for the few moments on King Street.

In the end, it was arranged that Kevin would come home for her, and take her to the Board to get her pay. With his uncanny way of knowing what was in Lucy's mind, Ross urged her to take time to go to the bank and also to take time to shop, if she needed to get things.

Lucy felt a bit foolish arriving at the door of the Board of Education in a limousine. To make matters worse, another security man unobtrusively followed her into the building and waited while she picked up her check. He accompanied her to the bank, also. Lucy could see that she was going to have no time to poke about the stores, but she did want to get something for Grandma Prentiss. She finally settled on running into a well-known candy shop for a suitable box of chocolates, and a drugstore for some Christmas wrapping paper and a card.

In spite of all the help from Kevin and his companion, it was well after three when she returned, and her charges were starting to get restless. Thanking Helen, she sent the children off to change into shorts and T-shirts while she hurried upstairs to find an old leotard. She prayed that Ross would not darken the doors while she was in the well-worn outfit, and hurried down to the great hall, as she sometimes called the entrance.

By the time the children had arrived, Lucy had some mats pulled out, the balance beam in place, and the mini-trampoline ready if she needed it. She had no intention of letting the children try anything fancy and was relieved to discover that they had only the vaguest idea just exactly what serious gymnasts did.

They started by practicing simple warm-up exercises and activities that stressed keeping the body in line, and then progressed to simple somersaults. From there, they moved on to the balance beam. Lucy was careful not to show off on the beam, knowing that it would encourage either foolhardy attempts at movements they could not do or discourage them because of the complexity of sophisticated moves. For that matter, Lucy was not sure just how good she would be on the beam; in the school's gym program, she had been too busy to practice her own skills.

The two children gave their best to each activity she introduced. Amy seemed to be a natural on the balance beam while Robbie took to the trampoline with ease. They were just finishing when Ross showed up in the hall. Embarrassed to be caught walking around in her worn old leotard, and feeling that she was exposing quite a lot of flesh, Lucy finished the lesson and casually put on her housecoat.

Ross was not fooled. He came over and complimented the children on their efforts, while out of the side of his mouth, he murmured, "Nice legs."

The rest of the day was uneventful. Ross had to go back to work, so Lucy and the children skated for a while after supper. Lucy was surprised when Robert Urquhart came out of his suite of rooms and helped Lucy get the children ready for bed. She found him a charming man whose green eyes were uncannily like his son's. He explained to her that he enjoyed getting the children ready and reading to them, but it was only now that he felt well enough to take up his old activities.

Lucy actually had time to herself when the children were tucked in, so she wrapped up her gift for Grandma Prentiss and made a list for Christmas. The children were easy. Robbie was crazy about hockey, so she would look for a book on hockey. Amy was still keen on learning to figure skate, so Lucy hoped she could find a book on the tiny American world champion Michelle Kwan. If she couldn't, she would try to find a sweater that would match the small skirt they had purchased at the sports shop. Even Helen was not hard to shop for. Lucy had noticed that she liked to read mysteries, so she would get her one of the latest in print and hope she had not read it.

When Lucy came to the thought of buying Ross or Robert a gift, her ideas dried up. To begin with, maybe it was inappropriate for her to give a present to her employer or his father. For that matter, if she gave them a gift, would they think she was expecting one in return? With disgust, Lucy put her list away. It wasn't supposed to be this difficult. The children certainly had no trouble making their lists. Why did she have to fuss?

Of course, the day was not complete without an hour of tae kwon do. Somewhat fatalistically, Lucy waited in her elegant room in front of the gas fire and tried to relax until Ross telephoned. When he did, he surprised her with a request. "Lucy, wear your leotard under your white outfit for me, will you? I want to ask you to do something."

When she entered the great hall, Ross was already warming up under the back-lit stained-glass window. Lucy often thought that the blond giant wearing the green, blue, and red kilt in the ornate glass picture with its Scottish crests, symbolic farmlands, industrial smokestacks, lumber trucks, and miners must be spinning in his grave at the sight of his great-great-grandson cavorting around on the mattresses.

When Ross made no mention of his request, Lucy settled down to work through the exercises with as much dignity as possible. Ross was a good student. Lucy figured he was one of those people who could quickly visualize a movement in his mind, for he only seemed to have to see an action once or twice before he was able to do it. He had worked himself through almost all the kicks, from the Roundhouse Kick to the Jumping Side Kick and was now eager to begin sparring techniques. Lucy was hard-pressed to keep up with him.

When he was finally satisfied that they had done enough, he pulled out the children's balance beam and turned it so that the large flat surface was up on the mats and the long, thin beam was up. Then he gave her one of those endearing grins that always seemed to rattle her. "Would you please do some of your balance beam exercises? I had a staff member go back and get clippings of you as a young girl just before you had your accident. You looked wonderful on the beam, as if it was part of you. I would be honored if you could do some for me. I think in some way it might restore my faith in beauty and goodness after these last few days of tension and danger."

What could Lucy do but comply, when his request was so gracious and full of need? Slipping off the loosely fitting white trousers and jacket, Lucy stepped carefully up on the beam and walked its length. It was slightly narrower than the standard gymnastic beam that stood almost four feet high instead of about fourteen inches. For a few minutes, she did no more than raise herself on her toes and settle back on her feet, work her arms and then her legs, one at a time.

Throughout all these movements, she was focusing, bringing her mind back to the series of muscle movements that permitted her to balance, leap, flip, and jump. Then, with a shy look at Ross, she stepped off the beam, went back to its head, and stepped back on it.

Ross was not prepared for the sudden brilliant display. One minute, Lucy was poised, tall, and elegant on the tiny width of wood. A second later, she was executing walkovers, flips, and handstands and then just as quickly, she was poised again as if she had never moved. The light from the window lit her chestnut hair, touched the outline of her delicate features, the gentle curves of her figure, and the long line of her legs. For one short moment in time, Lucy had seemed ethereal, soaring in the ether, a goddess of light and movement.

Then she stepped off the beam, grinned at Ross, and remarked prosaically, ''The beam is just a trifle narrow.'' Glancing up, she added, ''The beams above look just about regulation size.''

Her teasing did not stop Ross from walking over to her, taking her face in his hands as if he found it profoundly beautiful, and whispering, ''Thank you,'' then kissing her.

Her heart rate was already pumping from the unexpected effort on the beam. Lucy found herself unable to slow down her response to his kiss. All the lectures of the past twenty-four hours dimmed in her memory as she responded to him, and she gave herself to the kiss as unselfishly as she had given the small demonstration on the beam. When it finally ended, they were both trembling.

''Leave the equipment for the morning,'' Ross ordered. And then, smiling wryly, he added, ''Come, I'll walk you to your door.''

As they made their rather staid way back up the stairs to her room, they discussed the next day's activities in subdued voices while between them thrummed the vibrations of the kiss.

At Lucy's door, Ross surprised her by asking, "Did you enjoy putting up the Christmas tree yesterday?"

Lucy thought it had been self-evident. "Of course, I enjoyed it." She thought for a moment, then added, "It was kind of you to share the experience with me. After all, it was a very special family occasion." Then, in spite of herself, she said, "I think if I ever have children, I would want them to have a Christmas tree."

"I'm glad you were there, Lucy." And then he said, "There is just one thing I forgot to tell you about Amy."

Lucy's eyes flashed to his face. Was there something wrong with Amy?

"Amy," Ross continued, "still believes in Santa Claus. Believes with great determination in spite of all the evidence around her to the contrary. She still wants the white-haired old man to come down the chimney. She has not reached the stage in her maturation where she is able to extract the essence of Santa Claus and leave behind the fantasy."

Lucy found that statement confusing, but she understood what Ross was asking. "I won't destroy her belief in Santa Claus, Ross."

He touched her cheek, "I never thought you would. But I thought you should be forewarned.

Amy will definitely want to visit Santa at The Bay tomorrow. Robbie understands the problem and is very protective of her. I'll make sure the security people understand and don't put their feet in their mouths.''

He frowned. ''I'm not sure why Amy is clinging to this notion so strongly. Maybe it has something to do with having no mother. Who knows? Anyway, I'd just like her to be able to change her beliefs at her own speed.''

''I'll watch over her,'' Lucy promised, and she believed with all her might that she would.

It was decided that the children and Lucy should go shopping as soon as The Bay opened, so lessons were switched to a later hour. This time, Ross was taking no chances. He sent along a secretary he trusted implicitly to shop with Robbie while Lucy would shop with Amy. A driver would care for the car while Kevin and another man would spot the crowd. Fortunately, the children were unaware of all the extra personnel, and were ready to enjoy the expedition.

Lucy had never taken any interest in Santa Claus, so lining up with a group of parents and very small children was a new experience. She had to admit that the three- and four-year-old children were particularly delightful as they approached Santa. Some of them actually trembled with excitement and one little soul started to cry. To Lucy's surprise, Amy stepped forward, took the small child's hand, and led her up to Santa.

Robbie was first to speak to Santa. With a very serious expression on his face, he walked up to Santa Claus and seemed to do a lot of explaining. Santa shook his hand when they had finished, and waited for Amy to approach.

As Amy crawled up on Santa's knee and whispered in his ear, Robbie tugged Lucy's hand. "I explained to Santa Claus that Amy still believed he was real and asked him to be very careful what he said."

Lucy was deeply moved. She had not expected such an insightful and caring attitude from one so young.

The shopping excursion went off without a hitch. The children found what they wanted without difficulty. Robbie had extra things to buy because, as he whispered when Amy was at another aisle, "Grandpa and I get things for Daddy's stocking. Daddy fills all our stockings but, of course, Amy does not realize this. I have to get more things this year because Grandpa is still getting over his operation."

As they drove back home in the limousine, Lucy pondered about Santa Claus. Her father had been quite right in many ways. There had been every effort in the store to entice the buyer to spend money. And she had seen many parents buying very expensive presents when it was obvious that they could ill afford them. But Robbie and Amy seemed more concerned over finding exactly the right thing for the family and Helen, and were quite happy to purchase presents within their means. What was special about the children's shopping was that they seemed to get great pleasure from choosing their gifts and chatted all the way home about how they would wrap them.

When they arrived home, Lucy was surprised to see a large van in front of the main doors. As she entered the house through the garage, she noticed Kevin and his team seemed to know who they were. Arriving in the kitchen, she asked Helen.

''Oh, they're the professional decorators Ross employs to gussy up the entrance hall for Christmas. It's too big a place for the family to tackle. Go and take a look.''

The decorating team was just finishing when Lucy entered, and she had to admit they had done a wonderful job. At one side of the rectangular hall, a very tall artificial tree stood where it would in no way detract from the subtly lit window behind. It was decorated with tiny lights and a multitude of pastel-colored globes and bows. Lucy realized that at night, the lighter-colored ornaments would stand out against the darkness of the hall's wooden panels.

The team had created a real Yuletide effect by stringing garlands of evergreen up the stairs and across the minstrel gallery. Large bows with clusters of colored glass globes nestled in them. Where the struts crossed, an enormous bunch of mistletoe trimmed with evergreen hung. Masses of potted flowers stood in the darker corners of the hall, and in pride of place, a magnificent grand piano. Groups of chairs were set up about small tables. Each had its own decoration on it.

Lucy could not help but let out a whistle and nearly jumped out of her skin when a voice said, "It's quite a show, isn't it?"

She turned to see Robert Urquhart smiling at her. "Can you imagine how it must have been when this hall was built? Probably there were real candles on the tree and on the tables. There must have been staff with pails of water lurking about ready to douse the candles. I can never understand how any building survived the season back then."

His words conjured up an image of women in long gowns, men in evening dress, and servants in livery passing champagne. He was right. It must have been quite a sight. And the thought of Ross's party gave her a shiver of anticipation. Just how was she to fit in the group of executives and their families?

"Ross will only let us have a real tree in the family room, where you are aware there are more sprinklers than common sense. Here, he insists on an artificial tree. Also, it is much simpler to have these people put the tree up and after Christmas, remove it.''

Then with a twinkle in his eye, Robert said, ''I understand we have a date to go shopping tomorrow. Two of the security men have undertaken to supervise the children's skating tomorrow afternoon while we escape to the boutiques. They promised to bring their skates, so the kids should have fun.''

Lucy could not help a little frown. ''I'm not going to be able to avoid this, am I? I certainly can't figure out why Ross wants me there. He has enough people around playing spy without me eavesdropping all over the place.''

Robert smiled gently and walked Lucy back toward the corridor, his hand on her shoulder. ''My dear, I'm sure, in your heart of hearts, you know why Ross wants you there.'' With that, he left her to her own thoughts. Did she? If she actually played hostess, was she committing herself to a role she had never in her life envisioned?

After supper, Ross, the children, and Lucy piled into the limousine to visit Grandma Prentiss, suitably accompanied and followed by security people. Ross carried a small artificial tree and box of ornaments while the rest of them carried shopping bags overflowing with colorfully wrapped presents.

Grandma Prentiss was a tiny, white-haired woman whom Lucy judged to be well into her seventies. She was delighted to see the children, hugging them and drawing them into her small living room. She welcomed Lucy especially, and insisted they remove their coats and find a seat.

Her apartment was charming. On one lovely oval antique table was a collection of pictures, including her wedding picture where she stood proudly with a handsome, dark-haired young man. There were also several pictures of a long-legged young man who she identified as her son. She explained, sadly, that he had died a number of years before.

The children helped their grandma decorate the tree after Lucy and Ross had placed it in front of the living room window. Mrs. Prentiss, who insisted that Ross and Lucy call her Sadie, had been baking. On her small dining room table there was a feast of cookies and tarts. There were also two carefully wrapped presents for the children.

Lucy had been touched at the way the children had each reached up and given the old lady a kiss on the cheek when she had given them their presents. They had held them as if afraid they would break, and promised to put them under the tree. Then it was time to leave their gifts under Sadie's tree and depart. Lucy was pleased to hear Ross say that she would be picked up in time for Christmas dinner on the twenty-fifth.

On the way back to the house, Ross received a call from Sam Cowan. By the look on Ross's face, the news was not good, but he said nothing except that Kevin would take him back to work and that he might not make it in time for the evening lesson.

Lucy felt uneasy all evening, fighting down a feeling of foreboding. She was not sure what had started it. Was it Ross's grim look in the car? Or was it just the feeling that something would happen, something over which they had no control? Maybe she was just picking up Ross's sense of powerlessness.

Ross had not returned when Lucy headed upstairs for bed. Instead of being relieved that there were no lessons, she worried. After she had showered, she slipped into her nightie and a burgundy velvet housecoat, her one luxury piece of clothing, and waited before the fire, a book in hand. Not that she read it. Soon she gave up trying, and spent her time racking her brains for ideas for gifts for Robert and Ross.

Finally she had come to understand that a gift was a gift. There should be no worries about whether a gift was expected or would be accepted. If she wanted to give someone a gift, then it was up to her to present it with her heartfelt best wishes and forget all her second-guessing.

She was just about asleep before the fire when she heard a tap on the heavy wooden bedroom door.

Getting up, Lucy went to the door to find Ross, still dressed as he had been at Grandma Prentiss's and looking very tired and drawn.

Lucy did not hesitate for a moment. "Come in." And she led him over to one of the chairs by the fireplace.

Ross sat down, leaned his head back wearily, and sighed. Lucy sat opposite and waited. At last he spoke. "Someone got into the accounting systems of one of our subsidiaries. It would never have been discovered if that note hadn't threatened the company. The worst part of it is that whoever is doing this tried to make it look as if one of my most trusted executives was skimming off profits. It was only the genius of Sam Cowan's investigator that made it possible to find the hoax and see through the frame-up. Fortunately for Carl, my executive, we have unrefutable evidence that proves he could not have done this, not because I would be tempted to believe ill of him, but because the auditors would have had to be convinced."

"So you can add several more characteristics to your profile of this individual," observed Lucy.

Ross waited and when Lucy did not continue because she expected him to respond, he prompted, "Go ahead, Lucy. Let's hear what you think we have learned. It's helpful to hear another point of view. Sometimes, it gives me another angle on the solution to a problem."

Lucy shrugged. "Well, I've nothing brilliant to observe. It's obvious the person is an expert on the information highway, with expertise in accounting. After all, I don't suppose one can diddle books without having a really good understanding of the process."

Ross nodded. "What else?"

"Well . . . this person was able to get into your systems. I don't know much about how this works, but I would suppose he or she must have had access to your information. Maybe he or she works for you and holds a grudge against you. Have you investigated anyone you have fired, or for that matter, employed on contract?"

"Good deductions, Lucy. Sam and I have a team checking out those very types of persons at this moment. Any more thoughts?"

While they had been talking, a very clear sense of a certain type of mentality was starting to form in Lucy's mind and she was unable to quell a little shudder. Maybe this was what had been troubling her all evening.

"What is it?" asked Ross.

Lucy could not contain her reaction to the idea in her head. She got up and walked around her chair. Finally, she turned to Ross, her eyes large, their gray tormented with concern. "Ross, I think you need to be very careful. There is a meanness, a vindictiveness, to this person's actions that is quite frightening. Notice how she has attacked the things you value most: your children, your company, and even your most trusted friend.''

"You said *she*, Lucy. Why?"

Lucy was surprised. She had not realized she had used the pronoun but now she thought of it, it seemed right. "I don't mean to demean my gender, Ross," she explained. "But it is almost as if I can feel a female presence in these actions. There is so much hate and as I said, it is directed at what you hold most dear. I think such hate felt by a man would take a more physical form. The push at the subway, even the tampered brakes and the collision, seem like male reactions, but threatening the children and trying to injure one of your most trusted friends and colleagues seems a more female kind of revenge.''

Then with a shrug, she continued, "Male or female, I don't suppose it matters. What frightens me is the meanness of it." She watched him carefully as she added, "I think such a person would be quite ruthless if he ever got his hands on one of the children.''

Ross's face blanched at that. Lucy walked over to him and touched his cheek. "I'm sorry I had to say that, but that is exactly how I feel.''

He took her hand and pulled her down on his lap. When she had tried to resist, he said, "Lucy, don't pull away. Just let me hold you and feel your arms

around me for a moment and then I will leave. I
need to recharge my batteries. I need to sense your
kindness and goodness to try to blank out this nightmare.''

Trusting that he meant exactly what he said, she
put her arms around him and held him to her to
comfort him. After a while, he broke their embrace,
helped her up, and stood before her. ''You look
lovely in that burgundy gown, Lucy. I'll keep your
image before me tonight as I try to unravel this mystery.'' Reaching forward, he kissed her tenderly on
the forehead and finally, the lips, and left her.

Shopping the next day with Robert was quite an
experience. He seemed to have recaptured that sense
of purpose and aura of power that she associated
with Ross. As they drove along, she learned that his
wife had died just after Natalie's death. It had, he
observed, been a hard time for both Ross and himself. The children had been their salvation.

Robert knew exactly where to go. He had the
driver let them off along with their spotter *cum* pro-
tector in an exclusive mall called Hazelton Lanes.
Lucy had never had the nerve or the time to
window-shop there, let alone purchase something.
''Now, my dear,'' said Robert, and Lucy realized
that he used ''my dear'' in the same way Ross used
his grin. ''My dear, you will allow me to guide you
in this venture.''

The statement, not request, was accompanied with such a twinkle in his marvelous green eyes that Lucy had no heart to argue. "I will consider your advice, Robert. I appreciate you taking the time to assist me."

Robert seemed to know the owner quite well. In fact, it appeared they were in cahoots from the very beginning. "You phoned ahead, didn't you?" Lucy hissed when the woman greeted him effusively and led him to a selected rack of dresses.

Robert ignored her and instead, introduced her. "Elaine, I'd like you to meet Lucy, a very good friend of our family. She would like a gown suitable for the yearly Christmas party the company gives at our place each year. I know that you have helped my wife and Natalie select clothing for this event and thought you might be able to assist Lucy, as she has had very little time to spare. What do you suggest?"

Then, in case Lucy got too irked at his interference, he said weakly, "I think I should sit down for a few moments and rest. I'm just recovering from surgery, you know."

Lucy's eyes sparkled with annoyance at the old fraud, but what could she say or do? So with as much dignity as she could muster, she asked to see the gowns selected.

Lucy had worn her exhausted black dress, the only pair of decent pantyhose she could find, and her one pair of pumps. At the saleswoman's suggestion, she removed her jacket so that the woman could get a notion of her size. Without hesitation, the woman walked to the rack and selected a short, black gown. She brought it over for Lucy to examine.

"You are one of the lucky women in this world who can wear black. This gown should look magnificent on you. You have the slight figure and the height to do it justice."

Lucy reached out to feel the fabric. The matte-black material had a luxurious softness to it. Exquisite black beading patterned the neck and along the arms. "The dress is made from a superb silk knit," Elaine explained. "The beading is hand-done. Why don't you try it on?"

Lucy really wanted to root around the rack with its profusion of colors and styles, but something told her that the woman was right. The very simplicity would suit Lucy. And black was a color Lucy could wear.

Stepping into the dress was a treat. The lined fabric hung from her curves and caressed her legs. Mind you, there was not a lot of skirt and quite a lot of leg showing. Now she wished she had higher heels on her shoes, for the dress made her feel very elegant. As if reading her mind, Elaine showed up with several pairs of black patent shoes. "I'm not sure of your size, Lucy. Try these and see if any fit.'' *Of course,* thought Lucy crossly when she tried on the first pair, *they fit perfectly.*

When Lucy came out of the dressing room, Robert stood. Walking up to her, he took her hand and kissed her fingers. ''You look quite wonderful, Lucy. The dress shows off your own beauty rather than showing itself off.''

Lucy was embarrassed. She had never in her entire life considered herself beautiful. Yet looking in the mirror, the long-legged individual with the black dress skimming her frame did look lovely. Smiling shyly at Robert, she asked, ''Do you think this is suitable for Friday? You're sure the other women won't be wearing longer gowns?''

Elaine assured her that her gown was just right. Ready to take it and get out, Robert detained her. ''I think you should take a look at this dress, Lucy. It's just the color of your eyes.''

It was true. The dress he held was the color of her eyes but there was no reason why she should get another one. ''This dress would be most appropriate for Christmas Day, Lucy. And I would like to get it for you as a way of saying thanks for saving my son's life.''

When Elaine raised her eyebrows at this information, as Lucy was sure she was meant to, Robert went on to explain how Lucy was clever enough to figure out that Ross was choking before anyone else and took appropriate action. He did all this while making it seem that she had been dining with them rather than attempting to finagle a meal for free.

In the end she agreed to try on the gray-blue dress, and of course, it was perfect. She was left with no choice but to accept the gift graciously.

Elaine was not a boutique owner in the Hazelton Lanes for nothing. When Lucy finally left, she had been sold delicate stockings to match the dresses and appropriate costume jewelry to go with each of the dresses. Lucy considered herself fortunate that she had not come out with an entire wardrobe.

Instead of heading for the car, Robert steered her out of the mall and across the street into a hotel. "We'll be picked up in the car after lunch," he announced.

"But the children," Lucy sputtered.

"Never mind the children. Everything is arranged. We are going to have a civilized lunch and then I will return you to your charges."

Robert watched as Lucy made her way to their table in the hotel's best dining room. His son was going to get a treasure, that's if he was smart enough to win her. Even when she felt shy, as he knew she did at this moment, she rose to the occasion. Her green ski jacket over her simple black dress did nothing to lesson her grace as she moved across the room.

He watched her as she slowly relaxed over the meal. She was not a beauty but she had great bones and a well-shaped mouth. Her eyes, of course, were her best feature. Natalie had not been a beauty either. She had been as vivacious as Lucy was serious, gamine in appearance with her vivid blue eyes, freckles, and short, curly hair. Robert thought that Natalie would have liked Lucy and would have been happy that Ross had found her.

Shaking off his introspection, Robert proceeded to entertain Lucy until they reached the dessert. It was then that the conversation became serious. Lucy fretted, "I just hope that I can be of some help at the party. Ross wanted me to keep my ears open."

Robert smiled to himself. Lucy was still in denial. She was still refusing to consider that Ross wanted her to be by his side as his partner rather than as a spy.

"Lucy, you already helped immensely by drawing our attention to the wording of the letters. It's funny, but I have had the uneasy feeling that those words you pointed out are an important clue. Somewhere in my mind, they have rung a bell. I just can't make the connection."

"Ross and I were talking about the writer of the notes last night," Lucy said. "I was telling him that I thought there was something very female about the way the person has attacked the children and his closest colleague at work in spite of the fact that the other attacks seemed very male actions. I wonder if there is some woman in Ross's past who bears him a colossal grudge.''

Robert's face lit up with inspiration. ''That's it. No wonder Ross did not think of it. He was too young.''

Lucy shook her head. ''What are you talking about, Robert?''

Excitedly, Robert explained, ''When Ross was eight years old, just Robbie's age, he witnessed an armed robbery that resulted in a fatal shooting. Ross had a perfect view of the incident and saw the gunman clearly as he fled the crime scene. When the police converged on the bank, my wife had to confess that Ross had seen the assailant clearly and could probably identify him.

''A manhunt followed and by evening, the robber was found. Ross was able to identify the criminal in a police lineup.''

Suddenly, Robert seemed eager to leave. ''I'm going to take you home, Lucy, and then go to see Ross. If he is not available, I'll tell Sam. I think they should try to get their hands on records of that robbery. It's just possible it's connected. Maybe the robber is out of prison now. I know that he was sent down for life, but it's been almost twenty-five years, and I understand that sometimes the sentence is shortened.''

For the rest of the day, Lucy felt more at ease, as if Robert's idea somehow took some of the mystery away and gave a sense of control. Possibly the children picked up on her relief, for they were co-operative and enthusiastic about everything they did.

The children appeared to have the same drive as Ross, for they managed to pack in a gymnastics lesson and skating—both hockey and figure. Their final activity was to write a letter to Santa Claus. This idea came up after Robbie had asked what a fax was. When he understood, he decided it would be a good way to send a letter to the North Pole. He had said this with a perfectly straight face to Lucy while winking. He was sure his dad would send the letter for him. Remembering her promise to Ross to keep Amy's belief in Santa strong until she was ready to accept a more adult version, Lucy helped the children with their letters and promised to give them to Ross when he got home.

Ross missed supper again, something that was unheard of as far as Helen was concerned. Lucy could tell she was worried about the danger to the family and the upset in its usual routines, and did her best to cheer her up. She found that she missed Ross at supper, too. To make it worse, Robert had not come home. His absence suggested that they had indeed found a clue. She wondered if the elder Urquhart was ready for such a long day.

At ten that night, Lucy got out the gym mats and managed to move enough tables and chairs to make room for their tae kwon do practice. She was sure that Ross would make it back in time for their work-out unless there was a crisis. Meanwhile, she would work off some of the restlessness that had started within her again. Not having heard from either Ur-quhart was nerve-wracking.

For a while she warmed up, stretched, and did some basic leaps and twists. Then she pulled out the balance beam, and began to work seriously at her moves on it. Her short display for Ross had been somewhat foolish. A bit of showing off. She could have hurt herself because she was out of practice.

Lucy worked for over half an hour until she was tired and a little bored. She finished by walking, running, and skipping the length of the beam a num-ber of times, then sat down to do some gentle ex-ercises to ease her muscles.

Unknown to Lucy, Ross had watched from the minstrel gallery while Lucy had worked. Lucy's lovely movements had eased his heart. It was as if he had come on an oasis of peace, watching her precise yet graceful passes through the air.

When she heard him come down the stairs, she greeted him with a radiant smile. ''Are you ready to work? Where are your whites?''

He came and sat down on the edge of the balance beam while she finished her stretches. ''Not tonight, Lucy. I'm wiped. I just got Dad settled down. He has this notion that he can return to work a little earlier than the doctors say, especially after his inspiration this afternoon. It is my hope that he feels a little worn out and comes to his senses tomorrow morning.''

He stood and offered her his hand. ''Come over to the library. I'll light the gas fire and we'll have a nightcap. I could really use one tonight.''

He held up the burgundy housecoat for her to slip into, and waited while she tied its belt. Then he helped her slide the equipment away. ''Leave the tables where they are. I meant to have them moved for you so the mats could be used until Friday. The caterers can move them back then.''

True to the best movies, the library had a hidden bar and fridge behind a bookcase and Ross served Lucy some juice and himself a nightcap. Then they settled down opposite each other in the chairs by the fire.

Ross smiled at their choice of seat. ''We're learning, Lucy, aren't we? The sparks fly when we're too close together.''

Lucy blushed when he teased her about the irresistible attraction she was trying to control. She ignored the remark and demanded, ''Tell me whether Robert's idea was useful.''

''It may or may not be.'' Lucy felt a rush of disappointment at this. ''The robber's name was Peter White. He wound up being sent down for twenty-five years. Unfortunately, he died this past fall just a short time before he was to be released on early parole. So you see, he could not be the person threatening us.''

Lucy found herself searching for straws. ''Were there other robbers? Did he have family that might want revenge?''

''You are asking the same questions that Dad, Sam, and I asked. Sam is trying to track down his family, but so far has had no luck. He said he'd let us know the minute he has anything.''

Then, changing the subject, Ross said, ''I understand you and Dad had a very satisfactory time this morning. You were kind enough to make him feel needed when you went shopping and gracious enough to accept his luncheon invitation. It was just what he needed. He came into my office this afternoon looking about ten years younger. Thank you, Lucy.''

How did he do it? wondered Lucy. Switching things around so that it sounded as if she had done something wonderful for Robert when in actual fact, it was the two of them that had bought her clothes, and Robert who had treated her to the lovely lunch.

She found herself wordless, her eyes smoky with frustration. Ross smiled benignly, pretending he did not understand the glint in her eye or wry expression on her face.

Changing the subject before she could articulate her frustration, Ross announced, ''I think it's supposed to get warm, even rain tomorrow. Maybe it would be a good time for one of those field trips. How about the science center in Ontario? There are lots of things to do and the kids can work off some energy. Kevin could go with you and keep an eye on Robbie while you stay with Amy. There are so many activities and such crowds that I think one-to-one supervision is necessary.''

Lucy had to admit that it would be a pleasant change for the children to get out of the house; however, her heart was full of trepidation after the incident on the highway. Her concern must have shown because Ross added, ''I'll arrange for Kevin to drive a company van that has smoked windows. I'll also have some spotters as backup. Since I have made no mention of this idea to anyone, I don't see why it shouldn't be safe. The street outside the house is being monitored continually with cameras. We have seen no evidence of anyone hanging around. This person is very clever. Too smart to take such a chance after last Saturday.''

And so it was agreed that they would go on the field trip the next day, leaving at ten in the morning. Kevin would let Ross know when they were returning. If Lucy thought it was a good idea, she was to let the children have lunch at the center.

As they walked up the stairs to their rooms, Ross described the routines for Friday. The catering firm would arrive about two o'clock. John, his assistant, would supervise all the comings and goings, as would the security firm. A small combo would arrive about six and set up. They would go out and eat, and return later to provide music for dancing. A buffet was to be served at eleven. When Lucy asked about the children who were attending, Ross explained that it just so happened there were no really young children this year, so it had been felt by the parents, when asked, that the children coming would manage one late night. A room and supervisor was to be provided for any youngster who wanted to sleep.

As they parted at their respective doors, Ross said casually, "I've arranged for you and Amy to have your hair done and whatever else you ladies do before a party. I thought it would be a nice treat for Amy. This is the first year she has been really old enough to enjoy dressing up. Get her to show you her dress. It was purchased a short while before you came. She needs a haircut. They know that at the salon. Kevin and an associate will take you. Either Robert or I will take Robbie for similar trimmings."

Lucy went off to bed, disappointed that the mystery was not solved and disturbed at the growing parental role Ross seemed to be forcing on her. She was very fond of Amy but was afraid to form a bond that would hurt both of them when she had to leave after the mystery was solved.

*   *   *

The trip to the science center in Ontario went off without a hitch. Although there were many teachers with their classes visiting the center, there always seemed to be something the two children could experiment with or participate in. What was even more fun was that Kevin and Lucy had just as much enjoyment taking part in the activities. When they realized that it was nearly lunchtime, they decided to stay and eat at the center's cafeteria, much to the children's delight.

Stepping out of the van back at the house, Lucy was on top of the world. The kids had really had a good time and the trip had been quite safe. She was not prepared, then, for Helen's long face or instructions left by Ross that she was to go immediately to the library.

Lucy hurried across the great hall under the eyes of Great-Great-Grandfather Urquhart and wondered what could have happened. When she knocked and entered, she found Ross, Robert, and Sam before a television monitor.

Ross indicated a chair before the machine and invited her to join them. "We're just waiting for Kevin. When he arrives, I'll ask Sam to explain what is going on."

At that point, Kevin entered and settled in a chair to listen.

Sam leaned forward in his seat and spoke quietly. "As you know, Lucy, Robert remembered that when Ross was eight years old, he was the unfortunate witness to the end of a robbery turned murder. As soon as Ross was reminded of this event, he called me in. The three of us decided that the incident was certainly worth reviewing.''

Turning to Kevin, Sam said, ''I believe Ross brought you up to date with the latest events before you left for the children's field trip. At that point, we knew that one Peter White robbed a bank and shot and killed a customer, probably more by accident than intent. The most damning evidence used against him was given by eight-year-old Ross, who had seen Peter exit the bank firing his gun.''

Sam walked over to the machine while he continued talking. ''To our dismay, we found that Peter White had died of a heart attack just before he was to leave prison on an early parole, some months before his sentence of twenty-five years was up. We were afraid that our lead had become another dead end, but decided to follow up by locating any information about his fellow robbers and his family.''

Picking up a video cassette, Sam stuck it into the VCR. ''My researcher finally tracked down this rather disturbing TV news coverage from the time of the sentencing of Peter White. See what you think.''

With that, Sam switched on the machine. Immediately, the side of a Toronto courthouse was shown. Outside one of its exits, a number of cameramen and a few members of the public were hanging around. Then the side door opened and a young woman with a youngster about four years old exited, along with what appeared to be her lawyer.

Instantly, the camera panned in on the young woman. From her expression, it was clear that she was grief-stricken. An interviewer asked, ''How do you feel about the verdict, Mrs. White?''

The woman burst into an angry harangue. ''They sentenced my husband on the evidence of a rich man's son. Poor people don't have a chance against their interests.''

''But Mrs. White,'' the interviewer protested, ''your husband had a gun and he did rob the bank.''

''My husband is innocent. Only that rich man's kid said he was shooting his gun.''

The woman began to sob loudly and clutch her small child to her. ''My son is without a father now, and it's all that rich little brat's fault.''

From there, the interview became more and more disjointed and it became clear that the woman had no real grip on reality.

There were three other tapings of interviews with the woman, either through the trial or just after it. In each case she had her small child close to her. Frequently in tears, he was frightened and clung to her.

When the small news cuts had finished, there was a silence while they all dealt with the pain, anger, and lack of logic expressed by Mrs. White. What was even more disturbing was the absolute refusal on her part to acknowledge Peter White's role in the robbery and killing, and the degree of abuse directed at young Ross Urquhart.

"I remember those clips," said Robert. "I remember how I felt for the woman's grief while at the same time being very uncomfortable with the fact that Ross was being used as her scapegoat."

Ross took over at this point. "We think that the poison Mrs. White was spewing out before her very small and impressionable son could have created a mind-set in the little boy that, later in life, might influence his behavior. Unfortunately, the two of them seemed to have disappeared without a trace. Sam has his experts busy trying to track them down through public records, but so far there have been no positive results."

Lucy had watched the tragic videos with a sinking heart. There was so much hate emanating from the woman's words and expressions. As if reading Lucy's mind, Ross said to her, "You said you thought there was something very feminine about some of the actions of this person. Do you think it is possible that Mrs. White is behind these threats?"

Lucy found them all looking at her, waiting. Did she think Mrs. White was the instigator? She wasn't sure. As she had pointed out to Ross, there was also a very masculine set of reactions.

"I think," said Lucy tentatively, "it is possible that Mrs. White and her son may both be part of this, as I feel there is also a male component to these attacks."

Sam nodded. "I think you are correct, Lucy. If we are on the right track, then I believe we'll find both are somehow involved. I asked the criminal psychologist we contacted to view these tapes and go over the letters and events. He hopes to get back to me tonight or early tomorrow. Maybe he will have something useful to add."

The meeting broke up at this point. Ross came over to Lucy and asked, "How did the field trip go this morning?"

Lucy could say with all honesty, "We all had a great time, even Kevin and I. It's a great place to spend a morning. The kids are supposedly writing and drawing about their experiences. Helen, bless her heart, is checking on them." Then she smiled. "You don't know how lucky you are to have such terrific kids. I expect they are both working like fiends without supervision."

Ross's expression grew grave and his wonderful green eyes deepened as he considered her remark. "I know I am very fortunate, Lucy. They are wonderful kids and I love them very much. I would do anything for them."

As Lucy walked back over to them, the insecure thought crossed her mind. *Ross loves his kids. I know that for sure. Could it be he sees me as a possible mother for his children? Is that what is behind his assault on my very susceptible senses? Is he purposely confusing me, making me think the attraction between us is something special when all he really is looking for is a mother for his children?*

Lucy stopped before Great-Great-Grandfather Urquhart as she walked back to the family room. With a grin she asked him, ''What do you think, Great-Great-Granddad? Am I the victim of a bachelor looking for a built-in baby-sitter or is this truly love?''

The tenor of Lucy's thoughts brought her up short. She really did not know what she felt for Ross; Was it love? She certainly found him attractive. She liked his self-confidence and clear sense of purpose. She appreciated the tenderness and affection he had shown to her and his children. But love? Did she really feel love, or were her hormones just reacting to the alpha male like any other female on the block?

Lucy sighed. She certainly did not have an answer in her heart or her head. *I thought people recognized love at first sight,* she thought. *Why is it I haven't a clue what is going on in my heart?*

That night, Greg phoned to say he and Jane were looking around for something to do that did not cost a lot of money. Would they like to have some skating partners? Jane would like a figure skating lesson, too. She'd always wanted to learn to do one of those neat spins, to quote Greg.

Ross received this call through dinner, and had recounted it for Lucy with a great deal of humor, imitating Greg's voice and giving a skittish imitation of Jane trying to spin.

"Really, Ross," Lucy had laughed. "You would have been better to convince her that I could teach her how to do cartwheels or stand on her head than figure skate. My knowledge is so rudimentary that it is amazing I can teach anything."

In the end, the four adults and two children had great fun. Ross even learned how to do a simple spin. There was only only one bad moment when Greg made some remark about Santa. Fortunately, Lucy was able to skate him away from the ever-sharp ears of Amy and explain that she still believed in Santa Claus.

Seven-thirty on Friday night came far too fast. Lucy stood before the elegant Victorian mirror in her bedroom and wondered if the image looking out at her was really herself. A slim figure with long, long legs, a cap of polished mahogany hair, and a black, miniscule dress glittering with tiny jet beads stared back out of the mirror. She turned and saw that the neck of the dress dipped sinfully at the back while the beading glinted in a fine line all the way down her arm to the cuff. She touched delicate jet drops hanging off her earlobes and refused to acknowledge that the conspiratorial Elaine of the boutique had somehow arranged for the pair of exquisite antique earrings to end up on Lucy's ears.

A knock on the door ended Lucy's retrospection. Going over to it, she admitted an absolutely breathtaking Ross in dress suit and Robbie poignantly splendid in exactly what his father wore. The two of them stood at the door, proud as peacocks, with a blushing Amy in a delicate peach velvet dress with a creamy lace collar.

"You all look wonderful!" Lucy exclaimed, and welcomed them in.

Amy ran to her and whispered, "The lace collar came from a dress belonging to my great-great-grandmother. Do you like it?"

"Sweetheart, you look beautiful," Lucy said, and could not help but give her a big hug.

Turning to Robbie, she curtsied. "How handsome you look, kind sir!" and offered her hand to be shaken.

Blushing deeply, Robbie shook her hand gravely and said, "Lucy, you look very nice."

Just as gravely, Lucy responded, "Thank you, Robbie."

Then looking at Ross, who was openly admiring her, she asked, "Is it time to go?"

But Ross was not going to be dismissed so casually. Taking Lucy's chin, he gently turned her toward him. In a gruff voice, he said, "You look absolutely terrific, Lucy. We are proud to have you with us." And then, before the children, he leaned over and kissed her. Not a peck, but a kiss that stated his claim.

Confused, Lucy backed away, turned off the extra lights in the room, and with her head as high as she could hold it, led them out into the hall outside.

When they reached the great entrance, Lucy could see that John, the PA, had been hard at work. Soft music came from the piano, candles fluttered on each table, and a myriad of tiny lights cast a glow over the lofty room, making it reminiscent of a ballroom.

Helen and Robert appeared, and suddenly, people were at the door and John was announcing their names. Lucy noticed that each person or couple presented a card to John and were also perused by a very handsome Sam who just happened to be standing near the entrance. Several children came in with their parents and were politely welcomed by Robbie and Amy.

All the time the people poured in, Lucy found herself firmly fixed to Ross's side. She was never introduced as the children's teacher, just as Lucy. If any of the men even looked sideways at her, Ross's arm snaked out around her waist. *Really,* thought Lucy crossly, *how am I to circulate and listen if Ross keeps me glued to his side?*

She said as much to him and he rewarded her with what could only be described as a wolfish grin. "Lucy," he announced, "you are right where I want you." As he spoke, the combo started to play, and without skipping a beat, he murmured, "I'm sure everyone is here who plans to come. John can keep an eye on the door. That's what he's paid so well for. Come and dance."

Before she quite knew what had happened to her, she was spinning around the room to the most romantic of ballads. "I knew you would be a superb dancer," he whispered in her ear. Leaning back from him, she remarked dryly, "Physical Education grads can dance anything from the highland fling to the polka!"

That remark did not deter Ross. He held Lucy close in his arms and enjoyed every sinful moment. Unfortunately, even the devil in him that kept him teasing Lucy was not equal to his sense of duty. There were friends' wives, secretaries, and other office ladies that he should dance with, as well as his own daughter. Finally, he led Lucy off to Sam and said, "Here, look after her," and headed to Amy.

Lucy was incensed and tried to wiggle out of Sam's arms. "Sam, you do not have to look after me. I am twenty-five years old, a schoolteacher, and quite able to look after myself."

Sam laughed softly in her ear. "C'mon, Lucy. Don't be a spoilsport. I'm a widower and I never get a chance to dance with a beautiful young woman.''

Lucy laughed in his face. "You're just as bad as Ross. You like to have your own way and expect to get it.''

Sam twirled her around. "I suppose that's true,'' he replied. "But you will notice that it hasn't made any difference to Ross or me. We have still had to face tragedy and loss. So be nice to us both, Lucy. I'm sure you are what Ross needs. I know, too, that I could use someone like you in my life.''

Lucy stopped in the middle of the floor. "Sam! That's out-and-out emotional blackmail. Stop it. I don't want to think of Ross or your needs. It's not fair.''

Sam bowed to her. "You're right, Lucy. I am out of line. But I must say that Ross looks alive again. I guess I can't bear the thought of that hollow look returning to his face. Somehow, you have ignited something in Ross that has been dead for a long time.''

Sam cocked his head as the music changed tempo. "Listen, they're playing a samba. I bet you know how to dance it. Let's do it.'' Lucy could not resist. Moments later, they were out on the floor giving a first-rate impression of a floor show.

After that, Lucy drifted off to see how the children were faring. It turned out that Robert and Helen were sitting quietly in a corner watching nine young children play a selection of board games. When Lucy asked how it was the children were all so well behaved, Helen smiled and whispered, "Santa is coming later. They want to be sure they are on their best behavior."

Santa was coming. How were they going to manage that? Would Ross or Robert be the Santa? Maybe the long-suffering John got the job. For that matter, why hadn't Ross told her? On reflection, she had to admit that he probably thought she would not be interested. After all, she was the one who disclaimed any interest in Santa Claus.

Later, the caterers moved in. Tables that had held refreshments during the earlier part of the evening were now filled with delicious casseroles, salads, and plates of cold meats and breads. Immediately, the crowd headed for the food, and then back to their candlelit tables to eat. The children joined their parents, but Lucy was interested to note that they also kept a careful eye on the various doorways as if waiting for some special arrival.

Lucy sat with Ross and Sam. She had had no choice. They both came and claimed her. Just as she finished her dessert, she was surprised to hear singing. Robert got up, went to the door, and greeted a group of carolers whom Lucy soon recognized as some of the people from the church. The combo joined them and soon everyone was singing carols. Ross leaned over and whispered in Lucy's ear, "I wanted this to be a surprise for you. I always think the carols sound lovely in this hall."

Ross was right. Between the candles glowing on the table, the glittering lights on the Christmas tree, and the voices of the singers, Lucy felt as if she were captured within the pages of a Victorian novel.

But the surprise was not over. Just as the singing was about to come to an end, there was a commotion behind the Christmas tree and the carolers began to sing, "You'd better watch out; You'd better not cry . . ."

Lucy was watching Amy, who was the youngest of the children, and her eyes were bright with excitement as Santa Claus suddenly appeared from behind the tree. *Whoever it is,* Lucy thought, *he or she is really good.* The beard looked so natural; the voice was low and the ho-ho-hos just right. Even the oldest and most cynical of the children were fascinated, especially when Saint Nick started to dig into his great big bag.

There was a gift for each child present. As each child took the present and clutched it to them, Santa instructed them to take it home and put it under the tree. When Santa finished, the choir stood up and began to sing again, moving before the tree, thus allowing Saint Nick to slip away. The illusion was perfect, and Amy, quite overcome by the experience, climbed up on her father's knee to be cuddled.

Not long after that, the guests began to leave. As

one lady explained to Lucy, "Tomorrow night is Christmas Eve and we all have a lot to do before it is over. This was a wonderful party. It's nice to know we are not expected to stay to the wee small hours just to keep the boss happy."

People were getting their coats when Lucy heard Sam's beeper ring and saw him go to the house telephone and place a call. Minutes later, he said something to Ross, and then headed off in the direction of the library.

Lucy looked around for the children and could not see them. Only mildly disturbed, she excused herself from the party of people, wishing everyone good-bye, and started to look for them.

Her first thought was that the two children had taken their presents over to the family room to place them under the Christmas tree with all the other presents that had been accumulating there. But when she got to the room, there was no sign of them. She went to the kitchen where a security person was on duty and the caterers were just finishing up. Again, there were no children and no one had seen them.

Alarmed now, she was about to head back to the grand entrance to see if she had somehow missed them when it crossed her mind they might have gone downstairs to the basement. She dashed down there but again there were no children.

Rushing back upstairs, she hurried down the corridor and into the grand entrance with its twinkling lights, empty tables, and dance floor, only to find Amy sobbing in her father's arms. Concerned, Lucy approached them only to encounter a look of such disillusionment from Ross that she literally felt the force of it and faltered.

Sam was standing behind Ross, and when she came closer, Ross thrust Amy into his arms and said grimly, "Take Amy to the library, Sam. I want to speak to Ms. Allen alone."

His tone and words stunned Lucy. What was happening? Why was he calling her Ms. Allen?

Sam took the tearful Amy in his arms, and then said as he parted, "Ross, I really have to speak to you in the library as soon as possible."

Never taking his eyes off Lucy, Ross answered, "Not now, Sam. Get Amy out of here."

As the door closed behind Sam, Ross turned toward Lucy. His eyes blazed green fires of anger as he approached her. "How could you, Lucy? How could you do it? You promised."

Lucy shook her head in confusion. What did he mean?

"I-I don't know what you're talking about," she managed to squeak out. "What's happened?"

That seemed to enrage Ross even more. "You'd dare to ask what has happened when you have just destroyed a little girl's happiness?"

All Lucy could do was stutter, "Happiness?"

"Don't play me for a fool, Lucy," he snarled. "Amy told me exactly what happened. She said that you said that there was no Santa Claus. That Greg was Santa Claus."

"But I didn't know Greg was Santa. I didn't know who it was at all. How could I say that to Amy?"

Her question only made Ross angrier. "Are you calling Amy a liar?"

Bewildered, and still not making any sense of the situation, all Lucy could do was hold out her hands in entreaty. How could he think she would hurt Amy?

But Ross was not finished. "You can stay here tonight, but I want you out of the house by seven in the morning before the children wake up." And then shoving her away from him, he headed for the library, saying bitterly over his shoulder, "And to think I thought I was in love with you. To think I wanted you as the mother of my children."

He reached the door and with his fist, hit the door open and disappeared.

In the beautiful hall, the Christmas tree lights still glowing and the lights and bows of evergreen still twinkling up the stairs and across the minstrel gallery, Lucy stood, unable to think what to do or able to understand what had happened. All that really stayed with her were the words *"I want you out of this house by seven tomorrow."*

Ross, the man who had tried to win her heart over the past week, could think that she could treat Amy so cruelly? Amy, whom she loved so much? She shook her head in confusion, still trying to understand.

Unable to stand the sense of betrayal she felt, she gave a cry and headed up the stairs, across the minstrel gallery, and along the hall to her room. Closing herself in the room, she sat down by the unlit fireplace and rocked herself with grief. How could Ross think so badly of her?

Her life had been irrevocably changed by Ross and his children. The thought of leaving them without so much as an explanation or opportunity to understand tore her apart.

She was so full of grief that, at first, she did not hear the timid knock on the door. When it happened again, she looked up in time to see the door open and Robbie slide in. He seemed to understand her anguish, for he walked over to her and touched her hand. "Lucy, I know you didn't tell Amy there was no Santa Claus. I heard Greg do it."

Lucy tried to make sense of this. "Greg?"

"Yes, Greg," repeated Robbie. "He was really strange. He came up to Lucy in the family room with the Santa Claus outfit and beard in his hand and said, 'See, little rich girl. There is no Santa. Lucy asked me to tell you.'

"Amy just looked frightened, so he said it again.

This time, he shook the beard in her face and said, 'Lucy told me to tell you that there is no Santa Claus. That was me out there, Amy. *Me*.' And then he dashed out the corridor door. Before I could get to her, Amy had run back to Dad. I heard what he said to you.''

Robbie's little white faced was pinched with anxiety, his freckles standing out like small pebbles. ''I didn't know what to do so I ran back to the kitchen and told the security man that Greg was acting strange, and that he should tell Kevin, and then I came to find you.''

Lucy smiled into his serious little face. ''Thank you, Robbie. Thank you for believing in me.''

He patted her hand. ''Daddy didn't mean what he said, Lucy. I know he likes you a lot. And so do I.''

Lucy knew what she had to do. She had to go to Ross and Amy, and make it clear she had no part in spoiling Amy's belief in Santa Claus.

''Come on, Robbie. We'd better go and fix things up.''

Entering the library, Ross held his sobbing daughter and tried to soothe her at the same time that he tried to fight the pain of Lucy's betrayal. Sam's voice barking his name shook him out of his misery.

''Ross, I need you now.''

The edge on Sam's voice brought Ross over to where Sam stood with the telephone receiver in his hand. "Does the name Gregory Spencer mean anything to you?"

"Of course; he's Robbie's hockey coach. He was also Santa Claus tonight."

"Well, he is also Peter White's son. He and his mother changed their last name. Greg's first name was Frederick, and in all the old newspaper articles and news clips we studied, he was referred to as Freddie."

As the full impact of what Sam was saying clicked, Ross felt himself break out in a cold sweat. Could Greg, that nice young man who had managed to earn his trust, be the person threatening him? If so, where was Robbie? And Lucy?

"Sam, get on the blower to Kevin's team, and also see if you can get the police over to Greg's home. It's an apartment on Sherbourne Street, number twelve, I think. I'm going to see if I can locate Robbie."

When they had begun to talk, the urgency of their voices had caught Amy's attention, and her sobs had subsided. Now, as Ross strode out of the library and down the corridor toward the grand entrance, Amy clung to him, not quite knowing what to expect.

When they reached the door, Ross put her down and took her hand. They moved into the hall and began to cross it when a voice rang out, "Get your hands up in the air, rich boy."

Both Ross and Amy's heads swung toward the sound. There, halfway down the stairs, was Greg, holding a gun. It trembled in his hand as he repeated, "I said get your hands up," And with that, he started down toward them.

Before Ross could shove Amy behind him, she yelled at Greg, "Don't you hurt my daddy," and threw herself on to Ross's chest, her arms around his neck and her legs around his waist.

Upstairs, Lucy and Robbie had just come to the entrance of the minstrel gallery when they heard Greg's first words ring out. Without thinking, Lucy covered Robbie's mouth with her hand and pulled him back into the upstairs hall. They both stood trembling for a moment, listening to Greg and then to Amy.

Kneeling down beside Robbie, Lucy whispered into his ear. "I think I know a way to help them but I need backup. Do you think you can get it for me?" Lucy wasn't sure at all that the idea forming in her mind would work, but more than anything in the world, she wanted Robbie out of danger.

"I want you to go back to my bedroom and use the house phone to get help. Try the kitchen number or the garage if you know it. If not, try the library. See if you can speak to Kevin or Sam. Do not bother your grandpa.'' Robbie nodded. ''Tell them what you have seen. Ask them to get help but warn them that they are not to use their guns. Tell them that I think I can disarm Greg. Can you make them understand that?''

Robbie was trembling, but he nodded that he understood. ''If you get them, then stay in my room and lock the door. If you cannot reach anyone, then you must go by the basement to the other side of the house to get help. You must not go near the grand entrance.'' With a hug, she pushed him toward her bedroom and then hurried back to the entrance of the minstrel gallery.

Below her, she could see that Greg had come down off the stairs and taken a position right in the center of the hall, just ahead of the dangling mistletoe. Ross was standing, facing him, his back to the main entrance, and Amy still hanging on to him like a limpet.

Breathing a prayer of relief that nothing worse had happened, Lucy stood, taking in the scene, her mind racing over her options. Then, she stepped back into the hallway. Quickly, she removed her pantyhose and shoes. She would dearly have liked to remove her dress but the tenor of the voices seemed to be rising so she decided she would just have to make the best of a bad situation. Then, on her stomach, she inched her way out along the gallery until she was directly behind Greg.

Ever so quietly, she stood up, and stepped over the gallery railing to balance carefully on one of the metal struts that she had teased Ross about. It felt cold to her bare feet and slightly rough. Automatically she noticed that it was also somewhat narrower than the standard balance beam.

Ross tried to watch Greg and his trembling gun hand, and at the same time, talk him out of his madness.

"Greg," he tried. "Let me put Amy down so that she can get out of the way. It's me you want."

Amy was having no part of that, and yelled at Greg, "I'm not leaving my daddy. Don't you hurt him."

Afraid that she would enrage Greg, Ross tried to stop Amy's shouting by holding her head against his shoulder. As he tightened his grip, a movement beyond Greg caught his eye. He did not dare take his eye off the gun. Instead he tried hard to concentrate on the movement in his peripheral vision and still talk to Greg.

"Greg, please put down the gun. You have so much to be proud of in your life. Don't put it all in jeopardy by harming Amy or myself."

Ross could tell that Greg was not really processing what he heard. He was sweating profusely and muttering to himself, "Rich boy, rich boy, you killed my father."

Greg waved the gun, and as he did, Ross had a

chance to focus above and beyond him for a second. What he saw sent his heart tumbling. Lucy, her face absolutely without color, was standing on the metal strut in front of the gallery railing, one hand on it, poised, ready to walk. *No,* he prayed silently. *No, don't let her do it. It must be at least ten or eleven feet up in the air. She'll kill herself.*

And he knew then what his heart had known all along. Lucy had not hurt Amy.

Greg waved his gun again and Ross returned his attention to the trembling youth, but always with Lucy on the edge of his vision.

He tried another tack. "Your mother must be proud of you, Greg. You're a great success, a self-made man. You even did some work for Highland Industries, one of our subsidiaries. They thought you were great."

As he spoke, Lucy straightened. She was going to walk across the strut and drop down on Greg and there was not one thing he could do about it.

Greg laughed at Ross's last remark. "That's how I got into your systems." And then, slyly, as if testing, "That's how I found out your pal Carl was fixing the books."

Ross fought to concentrate. If she dropped, what could he do? He didn't want that gun going off near Amy. Could he time a kick if he was ready when Lucy dropped? Which kick could he manage and still keep Amy shielded? Maybe the Spinning Back

Kick Lucy and he had practiced. It was about as sane an idea as Lucy galloping across that blasted strut.

Suddenly, Greg snuffled. ''My mother died in November. Now I have no one. It's your fault.''

Greg's voice rose as he wailed out this information and Ross caught the frenetic quality of it. So, he could see, had Lucy, for suddenly, with arms outstretched for balance, she moved out across the strut, moved so quickly that she had little opportunity to lose her balance.

In the blink of an eye, she was just behind Greg. Then, feet first, like a diver entering the water, she knifed down, hitting his left shoulder so that he was spun sideways and down.

At the same moment that Ross saw Lucy leave the strut, he turned his body away from Greg and shot out his left foot behind him, deftly striking the gun just before Lucy sent Greg pitching forward.

Continuing the momentum of his turn, he completed it and couldn't believe his eyes. Somehow, Lucy had stopped her descent by catching the strut and was about to drop on a very confused Greg when Sam, Kevin, and several security people burst through separate doors and threw themselves on him.

Ross jumped around them at the same moment and attempted to grab at Lucy. The three of them ended up on the floor; Ross on the bottom on his back, Amy still clinging to him, and Lucy, caught by the waist, on top. Struggling to her feet, Lucy pried Amy off her father and handed her to Sam.

Then, she turned to Ross, who was struggling to get his breath and stand. At another time, she would have been indignant and wanted him to crawl to her for forgiveness. But at this moment, all she could think of was that he was alive and that she loved him with all her heart.

Leaning forward, she gave him her hand, and pulled him to his feet. For a split second, they stared at each other, and then they were in each other's arms, clinging to each other as if their lives depended on it.

Sam's voice brought them back to earth. "Ross, the police are here."

Ross, as dazed as Lucy, turned to see Sam, Amy still in his arms, inclining his head toward several officers entering the hall. Turning back to Lucy, Ross said quietly, "Are you really all right?" When Lucy nodded, he asked, "Where's Robbie?"

Sam answered for her. "He's upstairs locked in Lucy's bedroom."

Ross reached out and touched Lucy's cheek as if to assure himself she was safe and then said, "I'll see you later. I have to deal with Greg right now. Maybe you could tell Amy what really happened."

Ross took Amy from Sam and handed her to

Lucy. "Lucy just saved both our lives, Amy. I want you to go with her." With that, he left with the officers.

Lucy looked at Amy, searching her expression to see if she seemed to understand the night's events. But Amy had reached her limit. With a sigh, she cuddled into Lucy's shoulder and sucked her thumb, an action Lucy had never observed before. With a smile, Lucy walked up the stairs to her room, where she found the door locked. Tapping on it, she called, "Robbie. It's me. Everything is all right now. Let me in."

When he appeared at the door, he was still pale. "I did what you said, Lucy. I phoned Kevin and he told me to stay here." Then noticing Amy, he asked in a wobbly voice, "Is Daddy all right?"

Lucy took Amy over to one of the chairs before the fireplace and placed her against its soft arms. Then she knelt before Robbie. "Your daddy is fine." Brushing back his hair, she smiled at him. "You were a perfect backup. The men were at the doors ready the moment your dad kicked the gun from Greg's hand." Robbie's eyes widened at this. "Then, Kevin and Sam came in and took Greg away."

Turning to Amy who was sitting, listening, her thumb still in her mouth, Lucy said, "Amy. I did not tell Greg to tell you that he was Santa Claus."

Amy's eyes filled with tears. "He said there was no Santa Claus."

"Well, he's wrong," said Lucy, and suddenly, she found she believed what she said. "There *is* a Santa Claus. He lives in our hearts and every year, he asks us to help him visit as many people as possible in the world."

"But Greg was wearing his beard and red suit," she snuffled.

"Greg was one of Santa's helpers. Unfortunately, Greg forgot what Santa wanted. Greg is sick and could not finish his job."

"His job?" hiccuped Amy.

"Yes. His job was to help Santa by visiting your daddy's party and bringing gifts for all the boys and girls. Would you like to be Santa's helper this Christmas? I know some stockings you could help fill."

Amy thought about this for a moment and then nodded.

Lucy reached over and hugged her. "I'm so glad because I'm a helper, too. We can go out tomorrow morning and do some shopping to help Santa. Robbie can, too. Tomorrow, we can get some presents wrapped to put in some stockings for special people. Would you like that?"

Amy nodded again but Lucy could see she was fading. Picking her up, she winked at Robbie and said, "C'mon, you guys. It's time for bed."

Amy was asleep before they could pull up the covers but Robbie was far too excited to be dismissed so easily. So Lucy described the entire event to him, deciding that the truth in this case was more important than a watered-down version. After all, the little boy had earned the right to hear the full story, as he had followed her instructions so well.

When, at last, he had nodded off to sleep, Lucy returned to her room and changed into a comfortable shirt and jeans. She still had heard nothing from Ross. The euphoria felt when they had all survived Greg's attack had begun to dissipate and she began to worry. Had she and Ross really made up? Did he really love her? Did he understand how she felt? Had he really said he had wanted her for his wife? Did he know for sure she hadn't spoiled Santa for Amy?

Lucy could stand the suspense no longer. She headed for the library only to find it empty. She finally found everyone in the kitchen. Kevin, Sam, and one officer were still sitting with Ross at the kitchen table with coffee in their hands while Helen was cleaning up what had obviously been a small feast from party leftovers.

When they saw Lucy, Ross stood and held out a chair for her. Without being asked, Helen handed her a coffee and a plate of sweets.

While this was happening, Ross introduced her to the officer. "This is the young woman who risked a fall of about eleven feet to that tiled floor. She was a gymnast on the Olympic team and tonight gave the performance of her life.''

''I'll tell you, Jack,'' Sam said to the officer, ''I have never felt so helpless in my life. I could see Ross and Amy through the crack in the door. I could also see Lucy and thought she had just lost her mind. I had no idea she could walk that crazy strut. One minute she was poised at the railing, the next she was racing across the bar as if it was a foot wide, and diving down on Greg like a hawk.''

Embarrassed, Lucy sipped her coffee and tried to change the subject, but Sam was not to be interrupted. ''And Ross, what the heck did you do just as Lucy leaped off the strut? One minute you were standing there, Amy practically holding you in a death grip, the next minute, you did some kind of twirl, and your foot seemed to reach backward and lift the gun right out of Greg's hand.''

Ross turned to watch Lucy as he drawled, ''We can thank Lucy for that piece of fancy footwork, too. She has been teaching me tae kwon do.'' Then, without warning, Ross reached over and touched Lucy's left wrist. ''That looks swollen, Lucy. Did you hurt it?''

Surprised, Lucy looked down at her wrist. It was indeed swollen but she had been so busy all evening that she had hardly been aware of it. ''I think I must have done it when I tried to stop landing on Greg by grabbing at the strut. This is the wrist I injured before the Olympics. I think it will always be a nuisance. Anyway, I have not done any work on the uneven parallel bars in a long time, and my muscles are out of condition.''

Immediately Ross insisted that Helen bring an ice pack from the refrigerator for her arm. While the men chattered on, Lucy sat with it on her arm, sipping her coffee and becoming more and more despondent. Ross was sitting there beside her, gravely polite, but otherwise ignoring her. Had she completely misunderstood those few moments in his arms?

At last, the men went and Helen headed for bed. For one moment, Lucy was tempted to flee, too, but decided against it. This was too important. She wanted to know now just how things stood between them.

Ross seemed unduly interested in arranging the chairs around the table. Finally, he looked at her briefly and suggested, ''Let's go into the family room. There is something I want to say.''

Lucy's heart plummeted. It felt as if it had dropped to her toes. There was something he wanted to say? No touching. No ''I love you.'' Just something he wanted to say. Lucy fought tears as she marched toward the family room, head up, back straight. It was harder to do this than walk across the silly strut, she thought wildly as she reached the hearth and turned defiantly to face Ross. If he was telling her to go, then she was going to go with dignity.

Instead of saying whatever it was he wanted to say, Ross walked over to the window and stood, his hands in his trousers pockets, staring out at the winter scene. Finally, when Lucy could have screamed with frustration, he turned. "Lucy, I don't know how to say this."

Lucy gulped. Her worst fears were realized. He wanted her to go.

"I don't know how to ask your forgiveness."

For a moment, Lucy was simply confounded. What on earth was he talking about? And then she remembered. Amy, of course, and Santa Claus.

With a sigh of relief and a smile that would have blinded angels, Lucy walked over to Ross. Reaching up, she touched his face. "Ross, you're a father, a good father, and you had no reason to doubt Amy. Under different circumstances, we would have sorted out the misunderstanding right then. It was just bad timing. Sam got the news about Greg and that had to take priority. There is nothing to forgive."

Ross looked into Lucy's clear, gray eyes, bright as the decorations on the tree, with their deep blue band of color holding all the joy eyes could contain. Gently, he took her face between his hands. "I love you, Lucy. I need you in my life. The children love you and need you.''

She whispered, ''And I love you, Ross. I need you in my life. And I love the children. I thought I would die of fright when I saw Greg waving that gun at the two of you. I knew at that moment that my life would never be the same if something happened to the two of you.''

And then, they were in each other's arms, claiming each other with kisses and caresses. Reconfirming those unspoken vows they had exchanged amid the confusion in the great hall.

Much later, together on the chesterfield, Lucy against Ross's shoulder, they talked about Greg. ''I am not pressing charges if he gets psychiatric treatment. I figure that Greg was torn between what his mother believed and taught him night and day and what he knew of the real world.

''I suspect that she constantly kept at Greg about the idea of somehow getting even with me. The fact they stayed in the district and that Greg went to our church when there were several nearer his apartment suggests that. I suspect when she died, he found himself without emotional support, and snapped. He was admitted to the psychiatric ward of one of the hospitals, where they will give an evaluation.''

Brushing Lucy's shining hair back from her face, he kissed her forehead. ''I think there is too much potential there to write Greg off. I really believe he was the victim of his mother's refusal to face the truth. Time will tell whether he will be able to sort things out.''

Ross straightened and reached into his trousers pocket. Mysteriously, he pulled out a small, square satin container. ''It seems like in another life, but tonight when everyone went home, I was going to dance with you under that great bundle of mistletoe in the hall, kiss you until you admitted you were mine, and ask you to be my wife even though I had no idea how you felt.''

Taking a ring from the small container, he took her hand. ''Lucy, will you marry me? Will you be my wife?'' And before she could voice any concerns, he continued, ''I know you will want to achieve your career goals by teaching for the next few years, and I am sure we can manage while you do that. What the children and I can not manage is living without you.''

He held her hand and he held the ring, but he did not put it on her finger. Instead he waited.

Lucy took his hand and guided the ring on to her finger. ''I told you I love you, Ross. We were meant to be together. Too many things have happened to doubt it. I am honored to be your wife. I love the children and look forward to a life together with all of you.'' When he went to seal their pledges with a kiss, she put a finger to his lips and told him gravely, "I think you should know that Amy, Robbie, and I are Santa's helpers now, and tomorrow, we are going shopping to help Santa fill any stockings around here that have been missed."